Samuel French

The View UpStairs

by Max Vernon

SAMUELFRENCH.COM   SAMUELFRENCH.CO.UK

FOR PRODUCTION ENQUIRIES

UNITED STATES AND CANADA
Info@SamuelFrench.com
1-866-598-8449

UNITED KINGDOM AND EUROPE
Plays@SamuelFrench.co.uk
020-7255-4302

Each title is subject to availability from Samuel French, depending upon country of performance. Please be aware that *THE VIEW UPSTAIRS* may not be licensed by Samuel French in your territory. Professional and amateur producers should contact the nearest Samuel French office or licensing partner to verify availability.

MUSIC USE NOTE

Licensees are solely responsible for obtaining formal written permission from copyright owners to use copyrighted music in the performance of this play and are strongly cautioned to do so. If no such permission is obtained by the licensee, then the licensee must use only original music that the licensee owns and controls. Licensees are solely responsible and liable for all music clearances and shall indemnify the copyright owners of the play(s) and their licensing agent, Samuel French, against any costs, expenses, losses and liabilities arising from the use of music by licensees. Please contact the appropriate music licensing authority in your territory for the rights to any incidental music.

IMPORTANT BILLING AND CREDIT REQUIREMENTS

If you have obtained performance rights to this title, please refer to your licensing agreement for important billing and credit requirements.

THE VIEW UPSTAIRS premiered at the Lynn Redgrave Theater in New York, New York, produced by Invisible Wall Productions. This production played 105 performances. The cast was as follows:

WES. . . . . Jeremy Pope
PATRICK . . . . Taylor Frey
BUDDY . . . . Randy Redd
WILLIE. . . . . Nathan Lee Graham
HENRI. . . . . Frenchie Davis
FREDDY . . . . Michael Longoria
INEZ / REALTOR . . . . Nancy Ticotin
RICHARD . . . . Benjamin Howes
DALE. . . . . Ben Mayne
COP . . . . Richard E. Waits
SWINGS . . . . Anthony Alfaro, April Ortiz

THE VIEW UPSTAIRS premiered in the UK at Soho Theatre in London. The production was produced by Jack Maple and Brian Zeilinger for Take Two Theatricals and Ken Fakler with Creative House Productions; and Associate Producers Ben Lockwood and Sue Marks. The cast was as follows:

WES. . . . . Tyrone Huntley
PATRICK . . . . Andy Mientus
BUDDY . . . . John Partridge
WILLIE. . . . . Cedric Neal
HENRI. . . . . Carly Mercedes Dyer
FREDDY . . . . Gary Lee
INEZ . . . . Victoria Hamilton-Barritt
RICHARD . . . . Joseph Prouse
DALE. . . . . Declan Bennett
COP / REALTOR . . . . Derek Hagen

THE VIEW UPSTAIRS was developed with support from NYU's Graduate Musical Theatre Writing Program, Rhinebeck Writer's Retreat, and New York Stage and Film.

CHARACTERS

WES – (mid/late twenties) Up-and-coming fashion designer. Has a following.

PATRICK – (early twenties) Young runaway hustler. Sex, magic, whimsy, bell-bottoms.

BUDDY – (fifties) Resident pianist, Elton John-coulda-been. Married.

WILLIE – (forties-to-sixties) Might know all the secrets of the universe, might be in the early stages of dementia.

HENRI – (thirties/forties) Bartender. Tough as nails, no-nonsense, old-school butch lesbian.

FREDDY – (twenties/thirties) A construction worker by day, drag queen Aurora Whorealis by night.

INEZ – (late forties-to-sixties) Freddy's mother, makeup consultant, and cheerleader.

RICHARD – (forties) Priest of the Metropolitan Community Church. Can be played by a woman, in which case use the name **RITA MAE**.

DALE / REALTOR – (thirties/forties) Hustler, homeless, hungry for acceptance. Means well. Burns down the UpStairs Lounge.

COP / REALTOR – (thirties/forties) As seventies **COP**, corrupt, homophobic, and violent. As **REALTOR**, the human equivalent of an uplifting pharmaceutical commercial with horrible side effects.

ENSEMBLE / CHORUS – Other patrons in the bar who round out the community. Optional.

SETTING

The UpStairs Lounge, a gay bar in New Orleans, Louisiana.

TIME

The show starts and ends in the present day;
the rest takes place back in 1973.

AUTHOR'S NOTES

A slash (/) indicates overlapping dialogue. Generally speaking, it's a bar and people aren't waiting for their turn to talk.

Generally, Wes speaks at a faster quip than the other patrons in 1973.

Wes is someone whose point of view shifts rapidly, to the extent of almost seeming ridiculous at times. Within a couple sentences he can lurch from jubilance to depression, fury, arousal, comedy, and back. For much of the show he is more personality than person, which gradually gets stripped away but is something he can snap back into on a dime. He is allowed/meant to be funny, and the actor playing him can enjoy how horrible he is.

I think each character in the show is the star, in their own minds if nothing else. So – actors should take risks, make big, bold choices, and assert their presence in the room in their own unique ways.

While the action of the show all takes place in one room, during the songs we should feel like we are lifting off into a space of magic and fantasy.

It's the seventies, pre-AIDS, and all homosexual activity is illegal. We need to feel both the tension and release of that. Most modern audiences don't know/remember what real cruising and sexual exploration felt like, so remind them!

While it's important to carve out true emotional beats for the characters, never let the piece veer into melodrama. For example, Patrick has theoretically been dead for forty years by the time he tells Wes about the fire at the end of the show, so he's had time to process in a way Wes has not.

For the ending monologue, at some point in the future the politics might need to be updated re: children in cages, Vice President, etc. If there's an easy substitution, go ahead and make it. If more complicated, please get in touch and I can work with you to find a solution.

While there is no specific ethnicity indicated for Wes or Patrick, I *strongly* encourage theaters to employ diverse casting and not end up with two white leads. I think the love story between these two characters is more powerful with heightened contrasts; they are meant to yin-yang each other in energy/physicality/vocal tone/appearance, rather than being generational parallels. Also, chemistry between these two actors is important!

Because *The View UpStairs* is about gay history and community, I think working with queer-identified performers is valuable to the authenticity and artistic viability of the show. If that isn't available in your community and you've got a talented actor who is game to play and serving rough trade realness, go for it.

There is a good deal of action that can take place in the bar that is not indicated on the page. The bar should feel like a vibrant, high-energy, dangerous, exciting place to be, and we should get the impression that there are other unspoken stories and narratives occurring throughout the night. When characters are not in a scene, they're still living their lives – cruising, drinking, dancing, etc. I leave it at the discretion of the director to build these moments in, especially in the case of a "pre-show" before Buddy starts to sing.

Buddy can/should play light piano underscoring whenever it's useful. Band should rock tha f*ck out. Sanging > singing. Get that Rodgers & Hammerstein vibrato outta here!

The View UpStairs was originally performed in an intimate, immersive setting, casting the audience as patrons in the bar when they walked into the theater. This allowed for actors to ad-lib with audiences in a way that was often hilarious, and also made the fire sequence more immediate and terrifying. While it's possible to do the show in a proscenium, I think a semi-immersive or fully-immersive staging is a better fit for the material.

The UpStairs Lounge was "home" for many of the patrons who went there. I think it's important to find ways for the actors, creative team, and crew to feel at home in the set. For our first production, everyone brought in their favorite kitschy knick-knacks and we hid them like Easter eggs throughout the room.

Willie's grand monologue holds up the action of the show for no reason other than to be f*cking fabulous. For it to justify its existence, it has to be EVERYTHING. Scene-stealing. Insane, physical comedy, high drama, camp. Epic. It needs to feel like we're going to gay church and this is the sermon, even more so than the actual sermon. The "That's all!" should only be added in if the audience is gagging, in which case the actor should throw his hands up, take a bow, and bask. Otherwise, get on with it.

For Freddy's drag show, if you ain't got a cone bra that can shoot confetti, just do something similarly fun at the climax.

Some of you might have heard Patrick's song "And I Wish" from our cast album. We cut it from the original run because after the fire, having another ballad so late in the show was killing the forward motion of the piece. Please do not attempt to restore the song without permission from the author.

Finally, many of these characters are composites of real people who frequented the UpStairs, but out of respect and creative license I've changed names and certain details. It's super important, however, that audiences be given some kind of sheet with the hard facts of the UpStairs Lounge fire and names of those who died. I would prefer this be given out after the show rather than before so that audiences don't go into the experience anticipating tragedy.

(1973. The UpStairs Lounge, a New Orleans gay bar with eclectic décor at once elegant and extremely tacky. The atmosphere is a bit seedy; men in various states of intoxication cruise each other, dance, commiserate, laugh, etc. For most of the patrons, this is home. **BUDDY***, the resident pianist, smokes a cigarette. After a moment, he heads over to the piano, extinguishes the cigarette, and sits down to play. He flirts back with the men cat-calling him, takes a shot of whiskey, and sings.)*

[MUSIC NO. 01 "SOME KIND OF PARADISE"]

BUDDY.
IN THE SUMMERTIME HEAT
DOWN ON IBERVILLE STREET,
SEX AND INCENSE MIXED IN THE AIR.
MET A MAN WHO SHOOK MY BONES
WITH ONE PENETRATING STARE.
HE SAID, "NO REASON TO FEAR
BOY, YOUR MAMA AIN'T HERE –
COME HOME WITH ME INSTEAD."
AND IT WAS HEAVEN ON A LOAN.
WOKE UP IN A STRANGER'S BED
AND I SAID:

I THINK I FOUND SOME KIND OF PARADISE –
NO ANGEL WINGS OR FAIRY DUST,
JUST THE RUSH OF LUST

BUDDY, INEZ, FREDDY, WILLIE, PATRICK, HENRI, RICHARD & DALE.
BUT IT'S ALL RIGHT.

BUDDY.
AND THOUGH THIS PLACE IS FAR FROM HEAVENLY –
NO GOLDEN THRONE, THE ECSTASY'S
JUST TEMPORARY,

BUDDY, INEZ, FREDDY, WILLIE, PATRICK, HENRI, RICHARD & DALE.
> BUT IT'S ALL RIGHT.

BUDDY.
> I HAVEN'T SEEN HIM SINCE THEN
> BUT I'D BEEN BORN AGAIN:
> THE WORLD WAS DANGEROUS AND NEW.
> I CHOSE A FAMILY OF MY OWN
> WHO SHARED MY BRAND-NEW POINT OF VIEW.
> NOW YOU'RE –

BUDDY & WILLIE.	**HENRI & INEZ.**
ALL GATHERED 'ROUND	OOH
IN THIS KINGDOM WE'VE	
FOUND	
WHERE THE QUEENS AND	
CLONES COLLIDE.	

BUDDY.
> AND THOUGH IT REEKS OF CHEAP COLOGNE,
> IT'S MY FAVORITE ESCAPE FROM THE WORLD OUTSIDE.

HENRI.	**OTHERS.**
I THINK I FOUND SOME	I THINK I FOUND SOME
KIND OF PARADISE –	KIND OF PARADISE –
ANGEL WINGS	NO ANGEL WINGS OR
	FAIRY DUST,
ONLY THE RUSH OF LUST,	JUST THE RUSH OF LUST,
ALL RIGHT.	BUT IT'S ALL RIGHT.
AND THOUGH THIS	AND THOUGH THIS
PLACE IS FAR FROM	PLACE IS FAR FROM
HEAVENLY –	HEAVENLY –
GOLDEN THRONE	NO GOLDEN THRONE, THE
	ECSTASY'S
ONLY TEMPORARY, BUT	JUST TEMPORARY, BUT IT'S
IT'S ALL RIGHT	ALL RIGHT.
ALL RIGHT	ALL RIGHT. IT'S ALL RIGHT.
I THINK I FOUND	IT'S ALL RIGHT
SOME KIND OF	
I THINK I FOUND	
SOME KIND OF	

BUDDY, PATRICK, WILLIE & HENRI.	INEZ, FREDDY, DALE & RICHARD.
ALL RIGHT!	ALL RIGHT!
I THINK I FOUND SOME	I THINK I FOUND SOME
	KIND OF PARADISE
KIND OF PARADISE	NO ANGEL WINGS
	NO FAIRY DUST,
NO FAIRY DUST	RUSH OF LUST.
THE RUSH OF LUST	ALL RIGHT!
IT'S ALL RIGHT	
AND THOUGH THIS	AND THOUGH THIS
PLACE IS FAR FROM	PLACE IS FAR FROM
HEAVENLY	
	HEAVENLY
NO GOLDEN THRONE	
	GOLDEN THRONE
THE ECSTASY'S JUST	ONLY TEMPORARY BUT
TEMPORARY, BUT IT'S	IT'S ALL RIGHT!
ALL RIGHT	
	ALL RIGHT!
I THINK I FOUND,	I THINK I FOUND,
I THINK I FOUND	I THINK I FOUND
I THINK I FOUND SOME	I THINK I FOUND SOME
KIND OF	KIND OF

(The song ends and the **PATRONS** *applaud.)*

[MUSIC NO. 01A "PARADISE PLAYOFF"]

(The lighting shifts as **WES**, *a blasé hipster, enters the room. He is accompanied by a* **REALTOR.** *Both carry flashlights, which they shine on the walls and ceiling. 1973 and present day continue to co-exist without being aware of each other.* **WES** *notices burn marks on the wall, with growing outrage.)*

REALTOR. I can't think of a better way to celebrate pride than becoming a property owner.

WES. What the hell happened to this place?!

REALTOR. Oh.

> *(He giggles.)*

A *tiny* fire. Nothing to worry about.

WES. The photos you sent look nothing like this! I've already spent a small fortune –

REALTOR. So – you'll go to Bed, Bath & Beyond and get some new curtains –

> **(WES** *starts panicking.)*

WES. This is a disaster. I can't un-send the press release.

REALTOR. Why would you?! Front page of the *Times-Picayune*? *"Trendsetter or Troublemaker? A Prodigal Son Returns."*

> **(WES** *buries his face in his hands, makes tragic noises.)*

And this location? The French Quarter for your first flagship?

WES. I *had* to get out of New York; so cliché, so five years ago.

REALTOR. You're an influence, a *force* –

WES. Hellooo! It's *[year]*. Why sell couture out of a utility closet in Williamsburg, when N'awlins is vibrant –

REALTOR. Edgy!

WES. Soulful.

REALTOR. Rustic!

> **(WES** *shines the flashlight around, sees more damage.)*

WES. And busted as fuck. This is a nightmare. I want my deposit back.

REALTOR. Maybe we can do a little better – five percent off the listing price?

WES. My followers will annihilate you on Twitter. Not to mention my lawyers. Thirty.

REALTOR. This building is already way undervalued.

WES. And how long has it been on the market?? Should we Google?

(He takes out his phone menacingly. The **REALTOR** *changes tactics.)*

REALTOR. Look – if you want to change your mind I understand. A building like this requires vision – only someone *overflowing* with creativity and style –

WES. And you think I'm not??

(The **REALTOR** *shrugs, feigning ignorance.)*

OKAY fine. Give me the keys!

(The **REALTOR**'s *demeanor immediately turns bubbly.)*

REALTOR. Great.

(He digs out the contract, speaks lightning fast as if listing medication side effects:)

I just need your signature saying you've now seen the property in its current state, we're not responsible for any injuries which might occur – falling beams, head trauma, toxic mold, yada yada. And then we'll be good to go.

*(***WES** *signs. The* **REALTOR** *hands him the keys and bolts for the exit.)*

It's been a pleasure meeting you, Wes. I wish you the greatest success.

WES. Thanks! *Bye...*

(As he slowly walks around the space, we hear a very faint, far-away echo of a waltz being played by **BUDDY**.)*

[MUSIC NO. 01B "WALTZ ECHO"]

*(***WES** *pulls out his phone and begins to film a video for his followers.)*

Hi sluts, it's your girl, Wesley. I'm down in the south, yes it's all very tragic see?

(He quickly films the destroyed curtains sadly clinging to the windows. He flashes a big smile at his phone, then frowns.)

WES. Ugh!

> *(He immediately resets his pose and face, hits record again.)*

Hey bitches! It's me! Wuh-wuh-wuh-Wesley! So many of you keep asking me, *"Wes. How is your skin so goddamn smooth?"* And the answer is...snail mucus. From Korea. Very expensive, and *very* hydrating –

> *(He makes a noise of pain.)*

You sound like a loser!

> *(He stops, takes a deep breath, then resets his pose and face. He hits record again.)*

Hi everyone, it's your favorite failure. I don't know what the hell I'm doing with my life, but my cheeks are bronzed for the gods and I just bought a building.

> *(He looks around the room, depressed.)*

[MUSIC NO. 02 "#HOUSEHOLDNAME"]

Oh my god. What have I done??

> *(Throughout this song, he continues to explore the space, having unintentional encounters with the past: a **PATRON** dances on a chair, **WES** takes a photo of its charred remains; someone sets down a beer mug on the bar, **WES** jumps off of it, etc. There is fun and ethereal beauty to be mined from the two eras not seeing each other.)*

I HAVE A VOICE THAT TALKS TO ME
IN MY HEAD SOMETIMES
THAT SAYS, "WHY NOT DO SOMETHING EXTREME?
SHAVE YOUR EYEBROWS OFF, MAYBE BUY A BUILDING."
AND THIS VOICE THAT TALKS TO ME
IN MY HEAD SOMETIMES
SAID, "THAT'S FUCKIN' BRILLIANT, BUY A BUILDING!"
SO I BOUGHT A BUILDING...

WHERE THE MOLDY WOOD IS A DOG-SHIT BROWN
AND EV'RYTHING HAS TO BE TORN DOWN

AND PLASTERED OVER DESP'RATELY
THERE'S NO PLUMBING, NO WI-FI, NO FIRE ESCAPE
JUST AN ANCIENT, DAMAGED VELVET DRAPE
THAT'S OLDER THAN ME.

YOU CAN CALL ME DELUSIONAL
BUT I'VE KNOWN SINCE I WAS EIGHTEEN
THAT I WOULD ONE DAY BE THE FACE
OF EVERY MAJOR MAGAZINE
I DON'T NEED COMMUNITY
I DON'T HAVE TO BELONG
MY HUNDRED THOUSAND FOLLOWERS
ON INSTAGRAM JUST CAN'T BE WRONG.

> *(He pulls out a tiny vial of cocaine from his pocket and snorts a bump off his hand.)*

I AM TOUCHED BY FATE.
TO HELL WITH THE PAST, MY FUTURE'S GREAT;
IT ALL STARTS TODAY.
I'LL BE A HASHTAG HOUSEHOLD NAME.

> *(He takes a series of selfies, rapidly changing poses.)*

I HAVE A THERAPIST
WHO TALKS TO ME SOMETIMES:
"THE VOID YOU FEEL CANNOT BE FILLED UP
BY RESTYLANE, OR BUYING A BUILDING."
AND THE THERAPIST WHO TALKS TO ME SOMETIMES
ASKED, "DO YOU FIND YOUR LIFE FULFILLING?"

> *(He smiles and rubs cocaine on his gums.)*

SO I BOUGHT A BUILDING!

AND IT'S NOT THE LAP OF LUXURY
BUT A STEPPING STONE TO THE FANTASY
OF PARIS COUTURE FASHION WEEK.
IF YOU SQUINT ENOUGH IT'S ALMOST QUAINT,
IT JUST NEEDS A HUNDRED COATS OF PAINT
IN ORDER TO LOOK LESS...BLEAK.

AND THE REST IS HISTORY.
I'LL LAUNCH LIKE A CANNONBALL

I'LL MAKE A MILLION DOLLARS
AND I'LL PROVE ONCE AND FOR ALL,
THAT I'M NOT JUST A "BASIC BITCH,
ANOTHER WANNABE NOUVEAU RICHE,
TIPPING TOWARD A BREAKDOWN."
WITH MY HUNDRED THOUSAND FOLLOWERS LIVE-
     STREAMIN' ME
WHO'S LAUGHING NOW?

> *(He takes another selfie.)*

I AM TOUCHED BY FATE.
TO HELL WITH THE PAST, MY FUTURE'S GREAT.
IT ALL STARTS TODAY.
I'LL BE A HASHTAG HOUSEHOLD NAME.
A HASHTAG HOUSEHOLD NAME.
A HASHTAG HOUSEHOLD NAME.
A HASHTAG HOUSEHOLD NAME.
I'LL BE A HASHTAG HOUSEHOLD NAME!

> *(He rips the curtain off the wall. Light streams in, and suddenly the **PATRONS** in 1973 become aware of **WES**.)*

HENRI. HEY! GET THE FUCK OFF MY CURTAIN!

> *(**WES** screams in terror. Some of the **PATRONS** scream back.)*

FREDDY. Are we being raided?

HENRI. Are you a cop?

WES. What?

HENRI. ARE YOU A COP?

WES. No!

BUDDY. Where you from?

WES. New York.

BUDDY. Well how'd you get here?

WES. I don't know!

HENRI. I didn't hear the buzzer. Who let you in?

RICHARD. Who'd you come with?

WES. Um... Uh –

(He looks to the staircase where the realtor left, is confused.)

WILLIE. Are you trade?

BUDDY. Not with that costume he ain't.

HENRI. Did anyone see you come in?

WILLIE. Are you in the life?

WES. What life??

HENRI. Shake him down!

*(**FREDDY** and **WILLIE** start searching **WES**' pockets. **FREDDY** pulls out **WES**' iPhone and holds it up curiously.)*

FREDDY. What is this??

(Presses a button. He gasps.)

Oh my god it just lit up!

WILLIE. Quick Freddy! Give it here.

*(He throws the phone on the floor and smashes it under the heel of his boot. **WES** screams in horror.)*

WES. WHAT ARE YOU DOING?!

(He picks up his destroyed phone and looks at it in disbelief, distraught. He tries to turn it on. No luck.)

WILLIE. Destroying your surveillance technology! I'll have you know I was once interrogated in the Kremlin for thirty-eight days straight. And did I reveal any secrets? NEVER.

RICHARD. Son, you're here for the church service, right?

WES. *(Panic.)* Okay. I think my cocaine was laced with M-Cat and now I'm tripping BALLS; is there a bathroom? I need –

(He pantomimes splashing water on his face.)

Water!

HENRI. I'm afraid we can't let you in there 'til we know you're safe.

WES. What do you want?

RICHARD. A few more questions: Oscar Wilde? Or Arthur Miller?

WES. Um. Wilde?

WILLIE. Sonny...or Cher?

WES. Cher!

> (**RICHARD** *calls out to the room:*)

RICHARD. He's safe!

> (*Everyone breathes a sigh of relief.*)

> (*To* **WES.**) Bathroom's that way.

> (*He points to the bathroom.* **WES** *runs in.* **BUDDY** *starts to lightly play piano again as life in the bar returns to normal.*)

[MUSIC NO. 02A "BUDDY'S LIGHT UNDERSCORE"]

HENRI. Just what I need. First I get woken up at five a.m. by some guy, screaming on the phone saying I turned his precious Betty Crocker housewife into a bulldyke, I go downstairs to make a pot of coffee – spill it all over my favorite shirt, stepped in dog shit on the way here, and now I got *this* delusional fairy –

FREDDY. I think he's cute!

BUDDY. Are you sure he's safe. We've already got Dale, who we just barely tolerate. Last thing we need is another crazy.

HENRI. Who tolerates you?

BUDDY. Oh Henri. You know you couldn't live without –

HENRI. Without what? Having to watch a bunch of demented nellie queens getting drunk all day? Breaking up fights every Sunday Beer Bust, bribing cops from coming in here and bashing all your pretty faces?

FREDDY. What about Diana Ross night?

> (**WILLIE** *drapes the velvet curtain around himself like a dress.*)

WILLIE.
   TOUCH ME IN THE MORNING.

HENRI. Lord! I need to sell this bar and move somewhere far far away!

   *(Suddenly we hear **WES** scream from the bathroom. He runs out, followed by **DALE**.)*

WES. This person just sexually assaulted me!

HENRI. That's strike one, Dale. You know the rules. I told you if I caught you hustling again I'd have / to throw you out.

DALE. I wasn't hustling –

WES. You said you'd suck my dick for five dollars!

BUDDY. Five dollars? Dale, are you having a sale?

WILLIE. What do you expect? With this Nixon economy –

HENRI. Those pigs are begging for an excuse to shut us down. It's bad enough we're queer. And we're the only bar 'round here with black and white people in the same room talking, and they sure as shit don't want that either. Go ahead and prostitute yourself at any other bar on this block, but don't bring that crazy shit in here.

WES. Hold up. Nixon?? What year is it?

   *(Beat. **HENRI** sighs.)*

HENRI. 1973 wiseass.

WES. *1973?!* OHMYGOD I gotta text my dealer. These drugs are fucking brilliant.

HENRI. Drugs ain't allowed either!

WILLIE. Unless you're sharing.

   *(**HENRI** shoots **WILLIE** a look.)*

WES. But why 1973? Why *this*?

   (He takes a deep breath.)

You know what? This is like that time I got my Aspirin confused with ecstasy and woke up on a park bench in a zebra-print caftan with a bag full of cat food. I'm okay! I'm just gonna *roll* with it.

DALE. See Henri? The guy's crazy. You can't trust a word he says.

WES. At least my face ain't serving third-generation trailer park realness.

> *(He snaps and puts on sunglasses.)*

The library is open.

> *(**DALE** lunges at **WES**. He is restrained by the other **PATRONS**.)*

HENRI. *(To **DALE**.)* Hey! That's strike two. Pull yourself together.

> *(**DALE** skulks off. **WILLIE** triumphantly drapes his arm around **WES**.)*

WILLIE. *(Ecstatic.)* OH. I love New Yorkers! They're so bitchy. Henri! One shot for the newbie.

BUDDY. And bring me a beer while you're at it.

HENRI. Why don't you get it yourself, Mary?

> *(**BUDDY** gives a knowing look to the other guys, then struts over to her.)*

BUDDY. Henri. Can I get a kiss?

> *(He points to his cheek, makes smooching noises.)*

HENRI. I'm gonna hit you. Maybe it'll feel like one.

BUDDY. Come on Henri...etta!

> *(He grabs the drinks as **HENRI** throws a glass of water at him. He moves out of the way just in time and laughs triumphantly. **HENRI** growls in disgust, then goes to grab the mop. **BUDDY** hands **WES** the shot.)*

Drink up.

WES. What's that for?

WILLIE. *(Innocently.)* A rite of passage.

BUDDY. A little bathtub hooch'll put some hair on your chest.

WES. No – I lasered it off. It's gone forever.

BUDDY. Live a little.

> (*He clinks his shot glass with* **WES***, then downs it nonchalantly, like drinking water.* **WES** *eyes his shot suspiciously, then tries to shoot it back. A wave of shock ripples through him. It burns like hellfire. He makes the noise of a dying cat, coughing.* **BUDDY** *slaps his back and laughs.*)

Rumor has it Henri soaks the booze in an old boot Willie stole from some trick back in the fifties. Gives it that special flavor.

WILLIE. Fleet week.

> (*We hear the loud buzz of the front door.* **HENRI** *sets aside her mop and goes down the stairs to let the person in.*)

WES. What is this place anyway?

[MUSIC NO. 03 "LOST OR FOUND?"]

BUDDY. (*Sensually, with grandeur.*) Only the shittiest low-rent flea-ridden dive on the Lavender Line. In other words, home.

> (*He grabs* **WES** *and drags him across the room.*)

WILLIE THE WISE, IS OUR RESIDENT SAGE
AND HE AIN'T SHY ON GIVING ADVICE.
HE'S THE BIGGEST DIVA TO COME FROM THE SOUTH
SINCE GOOD OL' LEONTYNE PRICE.
NOW WILLIE MIGHT SEEM LIKE A SHADY-ASS QUEEN,
BUT HE'S REALLY GOT EVERYONE'S BACK.
AND HE'S A DAY YOUNGER THAN JESUS,

WILLIE.
BUT YOU CAN'T TELL 'CAUSE BLACK DON'T CRACK.

WILLIE & FREDDY.
BLACK DON'T CRACK!

BUDDY.
AMEN!

NEED A SHOULDER TO CRY ON?

BUDDY.

SOME DRUGS TO GET HIGH ON?
TAKE A LOOK AROUND.
JUST A MINUTE AGO YOU WERE LOST
BUT NOW YOU'RE FOUND.

YOU CAN

BUDDY, WILLIE & FREDDY.

FIND A NEW MOTHER
A FRIEND, OR A LOVER
STICK AROUND AND SEE!

BUDDY.	**WILLIE & FREDDY.**
JUST A MINUTE AGO YOU WERE BOUND,	OOH

BUDDY, WILLIE & FREDDY.

BUT NOW YOU'RE FREE.

> (**HENRI** *walks back up the stairs with* **PATRICK** *trailing not far behind.* **WES** *and* **PATRICK** *lock eyes for a moment before* **PATRICK** *goes to sit by himself at the bar.*)

WES. Who's that?

BUDDY. No one worth knowing...

FREDDY. Buddy, you're evil. I can't imagine what you say about me when I'm not around.

> (*He flutters his eyelashes.*)

BUDDY.

FREDDY MOVED HERE FROM PUERTO RICO
TO TASTE THE AMERICAN DREAM.
HE'D SPEND HIS DAYS WORKING IN CONSTRUCTION,
AND NIGHTS TRYING ON MOM'S MAYBELLINE.
IT WASN'T TOO LONG BEFORE HE GOT CAUGHT,
AND HIS FATHER CALLED HIM A DISGRACE.

FREDDY.

BUT NOW MY MOM COMES TO EVERY SHOW!

BUDDY.

TO MAKE SURE HIS TITTIES STAY IN THEIR PLACE.

WILLIE, FREDDY, RICHARD & HENRI.

TO MAKE SURE THOSE TITTIES STAY.

BUDDY.

IF YOU DESIRE A STRANGER,
A LITTLE BIT OF DANGER –

BUDDY & WILLIE.

TAKE A LOOK AROUND.

FREDDY, RICHARD & HENRI.

TAKE A LOOK AROUND.

BUDDY.

JUST A MINUTE AGO YOU WERE LOST

WILLIE, FREDDY, RICHARD & HENRI.

BUT NOW YOU'RE FOUND.

BUDDY.

YOU CAN

WILLIE, FREDDY, RICHARD & HENRI.

FIND A NEW MOTHER
A FRIEND, OR A LOVER
STICK AROUND AND SEE!

BUDDY.

JUST A MINUTE AGO YOU WERE BOUND

WILLIE, FREDDY, RICHARD & HENRI.

BUT NOW YOU'RE FREE.

HENRI. Hey! You forget about me?

BUDDY. You, Henri? Never. Shall I speak of your cheery disposition?

HENRI. Don't bother! I can speak for myself.

BUILT THIS PLACE TO FINALLY HAVE A HOME
AND I WORK HARD TO CARE FOR IT
I LOVE THIS WHOLE COMMUNITY
EVEN THOUGH YOU'RE ALL FULL OF SHIT.
THE SECOND TROUBLE COMES A'KNOCKING
ALL YOU FAIRIES'LL FLY OUTTA VIEW.
BUT I DON'T RUN, I GOT A MEAN RIGHT HOOK
AND MORE BALLS THAN ANY OF YOU!

HENRI.	**WILLIE, FREDDY & RICHARD.**
I'VE GOT BALLS.	SHE'S GOT BALLS.

DALE.

THAT'S TRUE!

BUDDY.

WANNA GO ON A BENDER

WITH A BULLDAGGER BARTENDER?

BUDDY & HENRI.

TAKE A LOOK AROUND.

WILLIE, FREDDY & RICHARD.

TAKE A LOOK AROUND.

BUDDY.

JUST A MINUTE AGO YOU WERE LOST

BUDDY & HENRI.

BUT NOW YOU'RE FOUND.

BUDDY.

YOU WANT A GLORY HOLE TROLL OR TO

DALE, WILLIE, FREDDY, BUDDY & RICHARD.

SAVE YOUR SOUL?

STICK AROUND AND SEE!

BUDDY.	**WILLIE, FREDDY, RICHARD & DALE.**
JUST A MINUTE AGO YOU	OOH
WERE BOUND	

DALE, WILLIE, FREDDY, HENRI & RICHARD.

BUT NOW YOU'RE FREE.

BUDDY.

THEN THERE'S ME, STUCK HERE PLAYIN' FOR TIPS

BUT ONE DAY YOU'LL SEE ME ON

BUDDY.	**OTHERS.**
JOHNNY CARSON, OUT AND PROUD,	OOH
UNLIKE THAT CLOSET CASE ELTON	CLOSET CASE
JOHN.	ELTON JOHN.
I'VE GOT MORE TALENT THAN TEN	WAH
OF THESE QUEENS COMBINED	
AND THE TRUTH IS I LOVE MY LIFE.	
I'M AT PEACE WITH WHO I AM –	

WILLIE.

BUT YOU'VE NEVER TOLD *THAT* TO YOUR WIFE.

*(Everyone laughs. **BUDDY** gives **WILLIE** some side-eye.)*

BUDDY.
NEED A SHOULDER TO CRY ON?
SOME DRUGS TO GET HIGH ON?
TAKE A LOOK AROUND.
A MINUTE AGO YOU WERE LOST
BUT NOW YOU'RE FOUND.
YOU CAN

ALL.
FIND A NEW MOTHER,
A FRIEND, OR A LOVER
STICK AROUND AND SEE!

BUDDY.
A MINUTE AGO YOU WERE BOUND
BUT NOW YOU'RE

ALL.
FREE.

DALE. Free to tell the world outside to kiss my –

*(He leans out the window and moons the people walking by on the street. People in the bar laugh, point, gasp, etc. **HENRI** snaps.)*

HENRI. That's strike three, Dale. You can waltz your bony ass outta here.

DALE. Oh calm down. It's free advertising.

BUDDY. There ain't gonna be a bar if the cops come.

*(**DALE** rolls his eyes. A phone behind the bar rings. Everyone gets tense. **HENRI** picks up, code-switches to a more feminine tone.)*

HENRI. *UpStairs…*

(She switches back to butch.)

Oh! Inez. Thank god it's you. I thought you were a law-abiding citizen calling to complain about the *ASS* hanging out our window. Yeah. He's here.

*(Shouts to **FREDDY**.)* Freddy it's your mother. *Again.*

(**FREDDY** *laughs apologetically and hurries to pick up the phone.*)

FREDDY. ¿Dónde estás?

[MUSIC NO. 03A "BUDDY'S TERRIBLE PLAYOFF"]

You were supposed to be here an hour ago. Okay okay! I'm coming.

(*He hangs up and goes to gather his things before leaving.* **BUDDY** *goes back to the piano and begins playing some New Orleans jazz.* **HENRI** *turns back to* **DALE** *disapprovingly.*)

DALE. (*Stammering.*) I'm sorry, p-please. Don't throw me out.

HENRI. I'm only giving you one last chance.

DALE. Thankyouthankyouthankyou –

(*He kisses* **HENRI**'s *bar.*)

HENRI. I expect you to be on your best behavior from here on out.

DALE. Scout's honor. Only the best! Cross my heart and hope to die?

(**HENRI** *wipes the spot he kissed on her bar and walks away from him. The other men in the bar dance, drink, flirt, cruise, smoke, converse, etc.* **WES** *spots* **PATRICK** *again by the bar, who smiles at him.* **WES** *snaps his fingers at the bar and makes a big show of flashing his cash.* **HENRI** *walks over.*)

WES. Here's a hundred. Let's have a round for everyone.

(*This stops* **FREDDY** *in his tracks at the doorway. "A hundred?!"*)

HENRI. HEY! Everybody. Drinks on New York!

(*Everybody cheers,* **BUDDY** *plays a rollicking pop tune in the style of Jim Croce's "Bad Leroy Brown." Everyone gathers around* **WES** *in celebration. They admire him like a shiny new toy.)*

[MUSIC NO. 03B "BUDDY'S HAPPY SONG"]

FREDDY.
My hero!
Are you single?

HENRI.
Finally some respectable clientele!

*(**HENRI** prepares drinks. **RICHARD** tells an audience member a secret.)*

RICHARD.
I knew those flyers would work!
All the young kids are at the baths these days.

FREDDY.
My mom would love you!

*(**WILLIE** crosses to **WES**.)*

BUDDY. Hey Dick, bring me a beer?

WILLIE. If only all the children could be so respectful of their elders.

*(**RICHARD** crosses to **WES**.)*

RICHARD. That's how you found out about us right?

FREDDY.
And that bicep!
Do you work out?

WILLIE.
No Freddy! He's mine!
I saw him first!

BUDDY. A beer! Are you hearing me or not?

HENRI. I'm going as fast as I can!

WES. Ladies please one at a time!

*(**BUDDY** slams his hands on the piano abruptly, stops playing, and gets up.)*

BUDDY. FINE! I'll just get it myself.

*(**RICHARD** grabs a beer for **BUDDY** to calm him down. They head off.)*

FREDDY. To be continued!

> *(He hands* **WES** *a bar napkin with his number on it.)*

FREDDY. Call me baby!

> *(***WILLIE*** *chases* **FREDDY** *out the room for stealing a potential date from him.)*

> *(***WES*** *and* **PATRICK** *are alone at the bar.)*

PATRICK. Hey big spender.

WES. What can I say? I'm very generous.

> *(***PATRICK*** *misunderstands the implication, flirts back.)*

PATRICK. Yeah...I can tell. I'm Patrick by the way.

> *(He holds out his hand for a shake.)*

WES. Wes.

> *(He touches it flaccidly, like it might lower his stock value.)*

Love your bell-bottoms. Very retro.

> *(***PATRICK*** *matches* **WES***' playful snark.)*

PATRICK. And where'd you get *this* jacket?

WES. I made it.

PATRICK. Really??

> *(He touches* **WES***' blazer, a little amazed.)*

WES. Do you like it?

PATRICK. It's incredible. I've never seen anything like it. It's so –

WES. Equestrian meets nineties rave meets Upper East Side housewife divorces her husband and eats pussy for the first time?

> *(***PATRICK*** *laughs, a little shocked.)*

"Uh –" I'm ahead of my time.

> *(***PATRICK*** *flirts back, playing to* **WES***' narcissism.)*

PATRICK. Creative, handsome, ahead of your time. Sign me up.

WES. You think I'm handsome??

> (**PATRICK** *gives him a look: "Obviously."*)

Trust me, I've spent enough time fixing my face on Photoshop. If my eyes were any farther apart I'd be a fucking hammerhead shark. Don't even get me started on my nose.

PATRICK. I'm sure the boys go crazy for you.

WES. Well I guess you've never heard the golden rule: No fats, no femmes, NO imperfections.

> (**DALE** *comes over. He tries to hand* **WES** *a beer.*)

DALE. Hey. I uh. Got you a drink. To apologize for before. We got off to / the wrong start –

WES. You got me a drink. With my money? Thanks!

DALE. Come on. I'm tryna be nice.

PATRICK. Piss off, Dale.

DALE. Yeah. Well, see you around.

> (*He walks away awkwardly.* **WES** *laughs incredulously.*)

WES. It's like I'm in a music video for the Village People!

> (**PATRICK** *is confused.* **WES** *sizes him up.*)

You know – you're pretty cute for a hallucination.

PATRICK. Is that what you're into? Picking up guys and then telling yourself it was all in your head?

> (*He leans in closer, hustling.* **WES** *gets nervous, starts to stutter.*)

Let's go to your place. / Shhhh.

WES. But. I – I. I haven't seen any photos of you!

PATRICK. You're looking right at me.

WES. I mean.

> (*He whispers, as if the word is too illicit to be said out loud:*)

Na-ked.

PATRICK. Well come into the bathroom. I'll show you.

WES. I'd rather not see it, until I've *seen* it and know that it's something I want to see. Besides, the last time I went in there I got assaulted!

(**PATRICK** *laughs.*)

WES. You think that's funny??

PATRICK. Take it easy. Outside of here we're *all* perverts.

WES. I'm not the one cruising for dick in the bathroom!

PATRICK. How do you cruise, Don Juan?

WES. You just do it on your phone. You say I'm Wes. Currently two feet away. Twenty-seven, 5'10", 140 pounds, and single. Looking for chat, dates, friends, masc, femme, white, black, top, bottom, whatever. You filter out ninety-nine percent of the people you *know* you have no interest in, and then after you hook up, you block 'em and they never bother you again.

PATRICK. Sounds like a bathhouse. Just a lot less fun.

WES. I wouldn't be going to bathhouses if I were you. It's not safe.

PATRICK. I'd trust a boy in a towel, before I'd trust a boy in a photo.

WES. Yeah well... History will prove you wrong.

PATRICK. What are you psychic?

WES. Uh-*yeah*. Ready for me to blow your mind? Nixon's gonna resign. Michael Jackson is going to be *white*, our president is going to be *orange*, and all of our personal data will float around above us in a giant invisible cloud.

(**PATRICK** *is confused, tries to readjust his hustle accordingly.*)

PATRICK. Oh...you like fantasy.

[MUSIC NO. 04 "WHAT I DID TODAY"]

Well – that's my life! Every single day: Magic. Adventure. Intrigue.

(*He winks.*)

It's exhausting.

TODAY I CLIMBED THE TALLEST TREE IN CITY PARK
AND SQUAWKED AT THREE OLD LADIES STROLLING BY
THEN I RAN TO CONGO SQUARE, WHERE JAZZ PERFUMED
    THE AIR
AND GOT MY PALM READ BY A VOODOO PRIEST WITH A
    GLASS EYE.
TODAY...

WES. I made a voodoo doll of my eighth-grade math teacher. Stuck a bunch of pins in it.

PATRICK. How evil of you.

WES. She deserved it. So? What'd the witch doctor tell you?

PATRICK.

HE SAID I'D BEEN A HERO IN ANOTHER LIFE:
MY ADVENTURES HAD INSPIRED SONGS AND POETRY
THEN HE SMILED AS IF TO SAY, I HAD GOOD JUJU
    HEADIN' MY WAY
AND HE WOULDN'T TAKE MY MONEY – HE JUST WINKED
    AND WAVED GOODBYE.
TODAY...

WES. He just vanished?

PATRICK. Poof! But that was just the beginning!

I JUMPED INTO THE BAYOU WITH NO CLOTHING ON.
FOUND GOLD HIDDEN BENEATH THE MUDDY FLOOR.

WES. All this in a day?

PATRICK.

I CLEANED UP WITH A COCKTAIL AT HOTEL MONTELEONE
RAN UP A THOUSAND-DOLLAR TAB, THEN WALTZED
    RIGHT OUT THE DOOR.
TODAY...

WES. None of this happened, did it?

PATRICK. Why do you care?

WES. I wanna know the truth.

      (**PATRICK** *reconsiders.*)

PATRICK.

TODAY I CLIMBED THE TALLEST TREE IN CITY PARK

PATRICK.

> GOT A TWENTY-DOLLAR TICKET FROM A COP.
> AND THERE WAS JAZZ IN CONGO SQUARE, BUT THE
>   VOODOO PRIEST WASN'T THERE
> I TRIED TO SING ALONG BUT THEN GOT ASKED TO STOP.
> TODAY...
>
> THE SUMMER HEAT BEAT DOWN LIKE HELLFIRE
> SO I SWAM TO THE SHALLOW DEPTHS OF A PLASTIC POOL
> WHERE THERE WAS NO GOLD. NOT EVEN A LITTLE BIT...
> AND IT'S TRUE THEY KNOW ME PRETTY WELL AT HOTEL
>   MONTELEONE
> 'CAUSE I'M ON A LIST THAT SAYS "DO NOT ADMIT"...
>
> BUT JUST WHEN I WAS READY TO WRITE OFF TODAY –
> I MET A BOY WHO SEEMED A LITTLE BIT LIKE ME
> A PRETTY BOY WHO HAD A MOST DISTINGUISHED NOSE
> IT WAS A LITTLE STRANGE BECAUSE HE DID NOT KNOW
>   WHAT YEAR IT WAS
> BUT I THOUGHT, "THIS DAY AIN'T OVER YET, LET'S SEE
>   WHERE THE NIGHT GOES."
> AIN'T IT FUNNY HOW FAST A DAY CAN CHANGE? FUNNY
>   HOW FAST...
>
> FUNNY...

> *(He leans in like he's going to kiss* **WES***, but pulls away at the last second to drive* **WES** *crazy.)*

Come on. Let's get out of here.

> *(***WES** *follows nervously until* **BUDDY** *jumps in.)*

BUDDY. Patrick! Is the newbie bothering you?

> *(***PATRICK** *buries his annoyance, tries to make* **BUDDY** *jealous.)*

PATRICK. No. We're – just leaving / actually –

BUDDY. Nonsense. You just got here. We haven't even sung our theme song –

> THE NIGHTS WE BRAVED TOGETHER LIVE ON INSIDE OUR
>   HEARTS

(To **WES**.*)* I wrote it. He loves that one.

PATRICK. Yeah. Well we don't got / time –

BUDDY. Don't want our new friend here to miss out –?

(To **WES**.*)* We sing it every night. You look like you appreciate tradition –

WES. God I certainly / hope not.

> (**BUDDY***'s over this game. He steps in front of* **WES** *to speak with* **PATRICK** *directly.)*

BUDDY. *(Cruisey.)* You know. I've been thinking about you... I get off in a couple hours. Maybe we could...for old times' sake?

WES. I thought you said he was no one worth knowing.

PATRICK. *Oh.* Is that / what you said?

BUDDY. Why don't you mind your own business? You think you can come here, start throwin' money / around – suddenly everyone's your best friend.

WES. O-kay. So much for your magical open community.

BUDDY. Who do you think keeps the lights on around here?

> *(Gestures to the audience.)*

Who keeps these people coming back night after night?

PATRICK. It couldn't possibly be the ten-cent beer.

BUDDY. You can get drunk anywhere. But you won't hear the original music of Buddy Straight.

WES. And what famous songs are those again?

BUDDY. Maybe you *should* leave. Before you wear out your welcome.

> (**RICHARD** *runs over to intervene, also carrying a vintage boombox in his hand.)*

RICHARD. Buddy! I think we're ready!

BUDDY. Thank you Dick. Excuse me.

> *(He gives* **WES** *a look, heads off.)*

WES. Bye Felicia!

[MUSIC NO. 04A "ABIDE WITH ME"]

(**RICHARD** *presses play. We hear the wail of a church organ come from the tape.* **PATRICK** *nudges* **WES**.)

PATRICK. Come on. Let's get out / of here.

(*Some* **PATRONS** *gravitate toward chairs to listen to* **RICHARD**'s *sermon. Others stand back, sip beer, and cruise. It's pretty weird.*)

WES. What the fuck??

WILLIE. Shh! Don't talk during the sermon. Unless you can hold a melody, in which case –

(*He sings with dramatic operatic vibrato:*)

SING OUTTTTT!

ALL.

ABIDE WITH ME. FAST FALLS THE EVENTIDE
THE DARKNESS DEEPENS. LORD, WITH ME ABIDE.

(**WILLIE** *starts to grandstand, shouting out gospel riffs, jazz scatting, etc.* **HENRI** *also starts to riff the house down, which puts* **WILLIE** *on the defensive.*)

WHEN OTHER HELPERS FAIL AND COMFORTS FLEE,
HELP OF THE HELPLESS, O ABIDE WITH ME.

WILLIE.	**HENRI.**
ABIDE WITH MEEEEE!	ABIIIIIIIIIIIIIDE WITH ME!

(**RICHARD** *has to intervene to stop the riffing.* **WILLIE** *is outraged* **HENRI** *would try to upstage him.*)

RICHARD. PLEASE be seated. Thank you all for joining me here on this lovely swelteringly hot summer day. I think we can all agree that, while God is perfect, the man who created polyester suits is deeply flawed.

(**WES** *makes the noise of a dying gazelle.* **RICHARD** *sees him.*)

You may have noticed we have a new member of the congregation. Our word is spreading. Hallelujah! What is your name, son?

WES. What? Oh. I'm not –

PATRICK. His name is Wes.

*(**WES** shoots **PATRICK** an evil look. **PATRICK** sticks his tongue out at him.)*

RICHARD. Wes. Thank you for your courage in joining us – For boldly standing up and saying your need to pray openly as a homosexual is stronger than your fear of being attacked.

*(**WES** smiles, terrified.)*

WES. Uh-ttacked?

RICHARD. In January, only a few months after we started our chapter here at the UpStairs, the Metropolitan Community Church in Los Angeles was set on fire and destroyed. If our congregation ain't safe out there, what hope do we have here in the south? Shouldn't we just shut down?

*(**WES** nods. Seems like the right thing to do.)*

But you said no! That the harder they strike us, the harder we will pray for serenity. The more they insult and reject us, the more we will pray for tolerance. That when our church burned down, the closet burned down with it and now we are filled with the courage to stand here proudly as God made us.

(Some applause.)

I prayed that our message would reach a younger generation.

*(**RICHARD** grabs **WES**' hand and holds it up triumphantly.)*

God answered my prayers. What will you pray for today?

[MUSIC NO. 05 "ARE YOU LISTENING, GOD?"]

WILLIE.

FOR KANDER AND EBB TO WRITE A SEQUEL TO CABARET!

BUDDY.

TO GET LAID!

HENRI.

TO QUIT SLINGING BEER AND GET THE HELL OUTTA
    HERE
TO LIVE MY LIFE UNAFRAID.

RICHARD.

FOR GOD TO INSPIRE AND PROTECT ME.

PATRICK.

SEE THE WORLD WHILE I'M IN MY PRIME.

DALE.

TO MAKE THE VOICE IN MY HEAD,
GO SILENT INSTEAD OF SAYING,
"IT'S FIGHT OR FLIGHT" ALL THE TIME.

BUDDY.

I PRAY FOR A MOMENT OF PASSING FAME
TO KISS MY WIFE AND NOT FEEL ASHAMED
TO LEAVE THE HOUSE AND NOT HAVE TO LIE

BUDDY & RICHARD.

TO BE MYSELF ONCE BEFORE I DIE.

BUDDY.	**HENRI, PATRICK, DALE & WILLIE.**
ARE YOU LIST'NING, GOD?	OOH

RICHARD.

HE'S IN THE CLOUDS, SO YOU BETTER SAY IT LOUDER!

RICHARD.	**OTHERS.**
HEY! SAY!	HEY! SAY!
RIGHT ABOUT NOW I	
COULD USE A MIRACLE.	
HEY! SAY!	HEY! SAY!
I DON'T CARE HOW BUT I	
COULD USE A MIRACLE.	
WON'T YOU GIVE ME A	WON'T YOU GIVE ME A
SIGN	SIGN
BECAUSE MY FAITH IN	
YOU IS FADING	

ALL.

I'M STILL WAITING...

(**WES** *gestures to a cardboard cutout of Burt Reynolds that hangs from the ceiling.*)

WES.

OH! IS THAT YOUR PATRON SAINT?
NUDE BURT REYNOLDS – THAT'S REALLY QUAINT.
IT'S PERFECT TO GO WITH THE MAGIC MAN
YOU THINK'S HOV'RING IN THE SKY.
BUT IF PRAYER WORKED I'D BE ON THE COVER OF *VOGUE*,
ATTRACT MORE TWINKS THAN KYLIE MINOGUE.
SURE AS HELL HASN'T HAPPENED YET
AND I AIN'T ABOUT TO HOLD MY BREATH.

ALL.

I PRAY TO FIND YOUR INNER LIGHT,
TO MAKE IT THROUGH ANOTHER NIGHT,
TO SHIVER WITH PURE ECSTASY,
TO FIN'LLY KNOW MY DESTINY.
ARE YOU LIST'NING, GOD?

BUDDY & RICHARD.

HE'S IN THE CLOUDS, SO YOU BETTER SAY IT LOUDER!

RICHARD & HENRI.	**OTHERS.**
HEY! SAY!	HEY! SAY!
RIGHT ABOUT NOW I	
COULD USE A MIRACLE.	

RICHARD & WILLIE.

HEY! SAY!	HEY! SAY!
I DON'T CARE HOW BUT I	
COULD USE A MIRACLE.	

RICHARD.

WON'T YOU GIVE ME A	WON'T YOU GIVE ME A
SIGN	SIGN
BECAUSE MY FAITH IN	
YOU IS FADING	

ALL.

I'M STILL WAITING...

RICHARD. Now, remember we have an important opportunity today to make a difference. Henri is passing around the collection plate for the Crippled Children's Hospital, so please give generously.

> (**HENRI** *passes the jar around. Over the course of the following exchange,* **PATRONS** *start to get riled up. Some clap, shout out.*)

DALE. Why the hell are we raising money for *crippled children*? They got parents.

RICHARD. We're creating understanding – making allies in the straight community.

DALE. Why is that always our responsibility?

WILLIE. Jesus turned the other cheek!

DALE. I'm sick of being the bigger person. I sleep on a bench in the park every night. How about a charity for me?

RICHARD. Our community isn't safe if we're isolated. At some point we have to build a bridge.

DALE. They will never accept us.

BUDDY. Speak for yourself, freak.

> (**WES** *grabs the microphone to hijack the argument.*)

WES. (*Faux-militant.*) Okay listen up *queers* –

> (*That word in 1973 has not yet been reclaimed, so it shocks the* **PATRONS**.)

If you're looking for acceptance, you're going about it all wrong.

> (*He switches to a sweet, if condescending, tone:*)

Charity and prayer is fine, noble…*but if you really want to change people's hearts and minds*…hire a publicist!

HENRI. OKAY! I'VE HAD ENOUGH BLASPHEMY IN MY BAR FOR ONE NIGHT. CAN WE HAVE A GODDAMN MOMENT OF SILENCE? JESUSFUCKINGCHRIST.

> (*As if on cue, we hear the sound of a police car siren outside. We see the flashing blue and red lights through the window.* **HENRI** *throws her hands in the air.*)

You're kidding me. What now??

DALE. It's a sign!

WILLIE. *(Worried.)* That's not the kind of miracle we were talking about!

RICHARD. It might not be for us.

> *(We can faintly hear the sounds from outside of a struggle between **FREDDY** and a **COP**, as well as **INEZ** pleading with him in Spanish.)*

WILLIE. It's Freddy!

> *(The front door buzzes several times.)*

HENRI. Buddy, put your wedding ring back on.

> *(**BUDDY** does as **HENRI** anxiously heads downstairs.)*

BUDDY. Okay everyone. This is not a drill. I'll handle the talking.

*(Singles out **WES**.)* Just keep your mouth shut.

> *(The door opens. **FREDDY** staggers in with **HENRI** and **INEZ** helping prop him up. He looks beat up – eye swollen, blood, etc. The other people in the bar whisper to each other, afraid. The **COP** enters the room.)*

COP. Hello ladies. Hands on the wall. IDs out.

BUDDY. Has there been a disturbance officer?

COP. Why yes in fact. Your friend Chita Rivera here was walking around in broad daylight with a wig on. Carrying two bags filled with women's undergarments.

BUDDY. His mother's I'm sure.

FREDDY. It wasn't just undergarments. You think I only wear panties onstage?

INEZ. *(Threatening.)* Mira! Stop making a scene.

COP. Hands on the wall. IDs out.

> *(He takes **INEZ**'s ID, reads it.)*

Inez Martin, forty-one. The degenerate's mother. Next?

> *(He starts checking IDs of some of the **PATRONS**. He writes down names. **BUDDY** approaches.)*

BUDDY. Officer. I have a wife and children. Trust me – there's nothing illicit going on –

COP. Then what's he doing here?

> *(He gestures to* **DALE**. **BUDDY** *communicates with body language to the other* **PATRONS***: "See. I told you so.")*

Picked him up a couple weeks ago: Prostitution, public intoxication –

DALE.	**BUDDY**.
I was just having a drink with friends.	He was just leaving.
I wasn't intoxicated! I had one beer!	

BUDDY. Look. We can come to an understanding, yeah? This jar –

> *(He grabs the charity jar.)*

Gotta be at least a hundred bucks in here.

RICHARD. We were raising money for the crippled children; spreading God's love?

COP. You ain't a real priest.

> *(He pushes* **RICHARD** *toward the wall.)*

I said hands on the wall. IDs OUT!

> *(***PATRONS*** put their hands on the wall.* **BUDDY** *grabs the jar for the* **COP***.)*

BUDDY. Anyway – I'm sure the children won't mind!

WES. *(Indignant, ridiculous.)* OH HELL to the no. I have to deal with this shit enough in real life.

> *(He gestures to* **BUDDY***.)*

Are you just going to let this coward sell you out? I thought these people were your friends?

> *(***BUDDY*** laughs at the* **COP** *nervously.)*

BUDDY. I'd hardly call these *perverts* my friends.

> *(***WILLIE*** makes a noise of indignation.)*

I just play piano on Sundays to make some extra money for the baby. I am not a homosexual.

WES. Oh please. Look at that silk handkerchief tied around your neck.

BUDDY. Will you SHUT UP? I'm trying to –

WES. Did you not hear the sermon? All of us need to rise up and –

DALE. Yeah! Go ahead. Arrest us!

> (**WES** *runs around trying to get people riled up. Some of the* **PATRONS** *respond: "Shut up." "Have you lost your mind?")*

We've got nothing to lose. Ain't that right Henri? Willie?

> (**WES** *ridiculously takes off his shoe, getting ready to throw it at the* **COP**. *No one is with them.)*

WES. Come on guys. I just watched that movie, *Stonewall*, on the plane.

> (*He suddenly speaks with an absurd Hollywood gravitas:)*

We can't let this happen!

WILLIE. Child. This ain't New York.

COP. I'm sorry. Am I interrupting something?

WES. Our taxes pay your income. So unless you want me to get your corrupt ass fired, I'd suggest you turn around, march back down those stairs, and –

> (*The* **COP** *grabs him by his hair.)*

Ow! You're hurting me.

> (*The* **COP** *whispers in his ear:)*

COP. You're under arrest.

WES. For what??

COP. Wearing women's clothing.

WES. Excuse me, my clothing line is gender fluid. It's not against the law!

COP. In fact, it is!

> *(He shoves* **WES** *into the piano. He sticks his hand into* **WES**' *back pocket and takes his wallet. He goes to cuff* **WES**.*)*

> *(***PATRICK** *grabs the jar from* **BUDDY** *and holds it out again for the* **COP**.*)*

PATRICK. Wait! Don't do this. He doesn't get how things work here. You've taught him. Now please – just let him go.

> *(The* **COP** *takes the money out of the jar, examines it.)*

COP. This is insulting...but I do think my wife might like that pin.

> *(He gestures to* **WES**' *lapel.)*

WES. FINE!

> *(He slowly takes off his brooch and holds his hand out for the* **COP**. *He affects a coquettish voice ala Anna Nicole Smith:)*

You want it?

> *(The* **COP** *goes to reach for it.* **WES** *grabs his hand, pulls him close, and kisses him on the lips. The* **COP** *throws him to the ground. He wipes his mouth, looks around the room, suddenly a bit afraid. Everyone stares back, shocked.)*

COP. *(Disgusted.)* You know what all of you do in here? It's sick. I'm coming back for every one of you faggots. So don't get too comfortable.

> *(He quickly pockets Wes' wallet and the money from the charity jar, then rushes to the exit. He knocks over a table on the way out. Once he's out the door there's a beat of silence, then immediately everyone launches into a frenzy over* **WES**' *action.)*

HENRI.

(Fed up.) That's strike number one *and* two for you! I swear to god I will kick your fairy ass to the curb before you put my bar in jeopardy.

BUDDY.

(Furious.) I told you to keep your mouth shut not to lock lips with the guy!

You could have gotten us all arrested.

Some of us have families to think about!

DALE.

(Excited.) Holy shit. Did you see? He kissed that pig!

The only thing worse would be kissing Henri! HAHAHA!

RICHARD.

I think we got through to him. It might not seem that way now but, he saw our generosity.

God works in mysterious ways.

WILLIE.

I mean I don't see what all the fuss is about. I've kissed hundreds of cops.

Wonderful lovers. So much aggression And handcuffs!

INEZ.

Uh. Hello? My son is bleeding.

He needs help?

Hellooooo?

*(**FREDDY** speaks above the frenzy, drawing attention back to himself in dramatic fashion:)*

FREDDY. Oh don't worry about me. I'm fine.

(He faints. The other men hold him up and grab a chair for him to sit in.)

INEZ. Somebody get him some ice!

*(**HENRI** grabs a glass and puts a few of the ice cubes into a rag. She hands it to **FREDDY**, who puts it to his eye. She also wets a cloth, which she gives to **INEZ**, who goes to wipe the blood from her son's face. While this is happening, **PATRICK** approaches **WES**, nervous and excited as if he's discovered a new species or color.)*

PATRICK. Hey – that was insane! You can't. I mean I've never seen anyone... Are you okay?

WES. *(Ridiculously.)* No I'm not okay! I just got hate-crimed –

RICHARD. Freddy, what happened?

FREDDY. Every. Single. Day. That asshole sits there parked on the same street calling me a sissy, spic, whatever – I don't care, but he has never said those things in front of my mother.

INEZ. Freddy, I don't listen.

FREDDY. He sees me in the wig, walks over, opens the trunk and says to my mom – "Can you suck dick as good as your son?"

INEZ. I hear nothing.

FREDDY. I said, "What do you care? You only like men anyway."

INEZ. It's my fault. I wish that I had more arms. Then I'd carry everything myself.

WES. This. Is. Ridiculous. If I was back home, I'd have this guy written up in the *Huffington Post* like that, the news would have a field day...

BUDDY. Leave the news out of it! The last thing we need is our faces on camera.

WES. Well there's got to be something we can do.

    (Silence. Beat.)

Anyone??

INEZ. We must pray that God curse this man.

WES. That clearly isn't working. Forget God! We're *gay*. We're creative! If you want allies – ENTERTAIN them. Give them something so fabulous and over the top it puts Mardi Gras to shame.

[MUSIC NO. 06 "THE WORLD OUTSIDE THESE WALLS"]

HENRI.

    YOU TALK LIKE YOU'VE NEVER SEEN

THE WORLD OUTSIDE THESE WALLS.
IN HERE, IT'S –

HENRI, INEZ, PATRICK, FREDDY & WILLIE.
SOME KIND OF PARADISE.

HENRI.
OUT THERE, YOU –

INEZ, PATRICK, FREDDY, WILLIE, RICHARD & BUDDY.
ROLL THE DICE.

HENRI.
THERE'S NO TRAMPOLINE:
YOU'VE GOTTA BOUNCE BACK UP ON YOUR OWN.
DON'T ACT SURPRISED!
IN THIS LIFE WE

HENRI & FREDDY.
FIGHT THIS FIGHT

HENRI.
ALONE.
I didn't spend years of my life turning this place into a home to see it get taken from me because of your stupidity.

WES. I was trying to help!

HENRI. Where do you think you are? The revolution ain't coming here. I've been gawked at, fired, spit on. You know how I fight back? By staying alive. That's all the revenge I need.
I'VE GROWN ACCUSTOMED TO THE VICIOUS STARES.
I BECOME A STONE WHEN I WALK DOWNSTAIRS.
I DON'T SCARE EASILY AT ALL.

HENRI & BUDDY.
YOU WON'T GET A STICKER FOR BEING NICE,
BUT NOTHING HURTS YOU WHEN YOU'RE MADE OF ICE.

HENRI & WILLIE.
FOR THAT STRENGTH YOU PAY A PRICE.

INEZ, RICHARD & FREDDY.
THAT'S JUST REALITY IN 1973.

HENRI.

> YOU BETTER STOP

INEZ, WILLIE, RICHARD & BUDDY.

> STOP

HENRI, INEZ, WILLIE, RICHARD & BUDDY.

> BEIN' SO WIDE-EYED.

HENRI.

> THIS IS A BATTLE

HENRI, INEZ, WILLIE, RICHARD & BUDDY.

> FIRING FROM ALL SIDES
> AND WE'VE ALL BEEN WOUNDED, SOME HAVE DIED.
> THE BEST REVENGE IS JUST TO

HENRI.

> STAY ALIVE.

ALL.

> THAT'S JUST REALITY IN 1973.
> THAT'S JUST REALITY IN 1973.

WES. And when that cop comes back tomorrow, or next week – you gonna keep buying him off?

BUDDY. Yes!

WES. Then nothing will ever change.

FREDDY. He's right. Next time that pig comes in here, I'm gonna throw my stiletto.

DALE. Gouge his eye out!

WES. Get him on film and leak his name to the press.

HENRI. Have you lost your minds? If they shut down the bar, where would you go? If they put our names in the paper, how would you find new jobs?

FREDDY. What have we got to lose?

INEZ. Everything!

> THE LAW IS BROKEN AND THE COPS ARE A JOKE.

FREDDY.

> THEY'D SOONER SIT THERE AND WATCH YOU CHOKE.

WILLIE.

> WE ALL GOT STORIES WE COULD TELL.

HENRI & BUDDY.
> I'D LOVE TO FLAY THOSE MEN ALIVE,
> BUT THEN I HEAR A QUIET VOICE INSIDE:

HENRI, INEZ, DALE & BUDDY.
> "KEEP YOUR HEAD DOWN AND SURVIVE."

INEZ, WILLIE, RICHARD, DALE, FREDDY, PATRICK & BUDDY.
> THAT'S JUST REALITY IN 1973.

HENRI.
> YOU'D BETTER STOP

INEZ, WILLIE, RICHARD, DALE, FREDDY, PATRICK & BUDDY.
> STOP

HENRI, INEZ, WILLIE, RICHARD, DALE, FREDDY, PATRICK & BUDDY.
> BEIN' SO WIDE-EYED...
> THIS IS A BATTLE FIRING FROM ALL SIDES
> AND WE'VE ALL BEEN WOUNDED, SOME HAVE DIED.
> THE BEST REVENGE IS JUST TO STAY ALIVE.

WILLIE.
> I'VE BEEN KICKED TO MY KNEES AND
> I'VE BEEN FIRED FOR NO REASON.

BUDDY.
> HAD THE WORLD SPIT IN MY FACE
> MY WHOLE LIFE LONG I'VE FELT OUTTA PLACE.

FREDDY.
> WE SHOULDN'T HAVE TO HIDE WHO WE ARE
> OR WATCH HOW WE DRESS.

FREDDY & INEZ.
> WHERE IS FREEDOM?
> WHERE IS PROGRESS?

RICHARD.
> THEY SAY WE'RE A THREAT TO THE WORLD DOWNSTAIRS
> BUT IF *THEY* KILL US

HENRI, INEZ, WILLIE, RICHARD, PATRICK & BUDDY.
> NO ONE CARES!

HENRI.
> I'VE BEEN ARRESTED, I'VE BEEN MOLESTED,
> LOST EV'RY PART OF ME.

HENRI.

YOU WON'T SURVIVE
IF YOU DON'T KNOW YOUR ENEMY!

(Ideological battle lines in the bar have been drawn amongst the **PATRONS.** *Old vs. new. Passive resistance vs. bold aggression, etc.)*

ALL.

YOU BETTER STOP BEIN' SO WIDE-EYED...
THIS IS A BATTLE FIRING FROM ALL SIDES
AND WE'VE ALL BEEN WOUNDED, SOME HAVE DIED.

HENRI, INEZ, WILLIE, RICHARD, DALE, WES, PATRICK & BUDDY.

THE BEST REVENGE

WES, FREDDY, DALE, RICHARD & PATRICK.

THERE'S SO MUCH MORE TO
LIFE THAN
STAYIN' ALIVE
UNTIL THE BITTER END

HENRI, INEZ, WILLIE & BUDDY.

IS
JUST TO
STAY ALIVE

HENRI, WES, FREDDY, DALE, RICHARD & PATRICK.

NO CRISIS HOTLINE

YOU ARE YOUR OWN BEST
FRIEND

INEZ, WILLIE & BUDDY.

UNTIL THE BITTER

END
HELLO HOTLINE?

YOUR OWN
BEST FRIEND

HENRI.

YOUR HEAD'S ON THE CHOPPING BLOCK LIKE ANNE
BOLEYN

HENRI, BUDDY, WILLIE & INEZ.

TOUGHEN UP NOW,

ALL.

GROW A THICKER SKIN.

WILLIE & INEZ.

DOWN HERE IN NEW ORLEANS,

HENRI, WILLIE & INEZ.
> IF THE COPS COME, HIDE YOUR I.D.

HENRI, BUDDY, WILLIE & INEZ.
> THEY'LL PUT YOUR NAME IN THE PAPER:
> "CRIMES AGAINST NATURE" FOR ALL TO SEE.
> YOU'LL LOSE YOUR JOB, YOUR LIFE, YOUR LAST STITCH OF
>   PRIVACY.

HENRI.
> AND THAT'S JUST REALITY IN 1973.

DALE. Well, that's your reality, but it'll never be mine!

> *(Some* **PATRONS** *cheer to support* **DALE**.*)*

FREDDY. *Wow*, Dale – for once we agree.

WILLIE. Says the girl with a black eye and a concussion.

> *(Some* **PATRONS** *whistle, sass* **FREDDY** *back.)*

RICHARD. Enough! We have too many people against us to be against each other. There's important work to be done. We can still raise some money –

> *(***DALE** *goes to mutter a protest, but* **RICHARD** *talks over him:)*

It's not just good for the people outside, it's good for us – *our* spirit, *our* community. And OUR community came to see a drag show.

FREDDY. What am I going to wear? He stole my hair, my brand-new Maybelline blusher, everything.

INEZ. Not everything!

> *(Like a clown car, she pulls out a blonde wig and a bag of makeup miraculously stuffed into her own outfit.)*

I've got concealer.

FREDDY. But I have no dress! You want me to look like a butch queen??

HENRI. You got a problem with butch??

DALE. You oughta stick a firecracker up your ass and light it onstage.

(He laughs as if he assumes others will join.)

DALE. I mean if you want people to pay to watch.

INEZ. How dare you speak to my son that way. Freddy is an artist!

WES. Don't worry boo, I got your gown.

(Shouts across the room.) Henri! Do you have a sewing kit?

HENRI. *(Annoyed.)* I have duct tape.

WES. Let's do this!

[MUSIC NO. 06A "DRESS PANIC"]

*(**HENRI** holds up the roll. **WES** grabs it. People in the bar cheer. **WES** goes to grab the velvet curtain he ripped off the wall before. **HENRI** screams:)*

HENRI. NOT THE CURTAIN.

*(Too late. **HENRI** sighs.)*

WES. And I'll take this, and these, and oh – sorry just gonna have to borrow this, and – yep! Definitely need these.

(He grabs a bunch of random crap from around the room to make the dress.)

I love this! I feel like I'm on *Project Runway*.

PATRICK. What's project –?

WES. Never mind. Let's go!

*(**WES, PATRICK, INEZ,** and **FREDDY** all run to the private corner of the bar. Scene transition. **INEZ** is helping **FREDDY** get into drag. She energetically beats at his face with a makeup brush while **WES** and **PATRICK** work on the dress.)*

[MUSIC NO. 07 "COMPLETELY OVERDONE"]

INEZ. Ay! Dios mio! This is amazing. I have never seen such a beautiful pink. What is this called?

(She looks at the bottom of the eyeshadow container.)

FREDDY. *(Dejected.) Damsel.*

> *(***INEZ*** *shrugs.)*

INEZ.

> IT'S MODEST AND SWEET, AND IT GLOWS ON YOUR FACE
> YOU LOOK LIKE A GIRL BLESSED WITH GOD-GIVEN GRACE
> NOT LIKE OTHER WOMEN, WITH THEIR LEGS SPREAD
> > EVERY WHICH WAY!
>
> > *(She seductively demonstrates, horrifying* **FREDDY**. *She immediately snaps back to herself.)*
>
> YOU REMIND ME OF ME ON MY WEDDING DAY.

FREDDY. Oh god. Mama! That is not the look I'm going for.

INEZ. It's a good look.

FREDDY. Yes, but where is the drama?

INEZ. Drama? Okay.

> HOW 'BOUT
>
> > *(She goes to work on* **FREDDY***'s eyes.)*
>
> I PENCIL YOUR EYEBROW LIKE LUPE VÉLEZ
> WITH LASHES AS LONG AS MARIA MONTEZ
> ELEGANT LADIES, WHO LIGHT UP THE SILVER SCREEN

FREDDY.

> THAT ISN'T THE DRAMA I MEAN!
>
> > *(***INEZ*** *plucks his eyebrow with a tweezer.)*
>
> Ow! What the hell?

INEZ. Beauty comes with pain.

FREDDY. I've had enough pain for one day. Ahh!

> > *(He tries to push away the tweezer, but* **INEZ** *is relentless. He continues to make sounds of pain while she sings.)*

INEZ.	**FREDDY**.
I ALWAYS KNEW I WOULD MAKE A GOOD MOTHER	*OW!!*
I PRAYED FOR THIS MOMENT TO BE	AHHHH

INEZ.	FREDDY.
GOD ANSWERED MY PRAYER, BUT WHY IS IT FAIR MY SON LOOKS BETTER IN MAKEUP THAN ME?	Ow. Ow. Ow.

FREDDY. Can I look already?

> (**INEZ** gestures to **FREDDY**, who looks into a hand mirror. He lets out a blood-curdling scream.)

I look so...mature.

INEZ. And what is wrong with that??

FREDDY. I was thinking more sexy hooker.

> (**INEZ** gasps.)

That came out wrong.

INEZ. No, I understand. This world is full of stupid men, and you want to look like a stupid woman.

> (She grumbles to herself in Spanish under her breath.)

> (**FREDDY** mouths along as he's heard her say it a hundred times.)

FREDDY. I heard that!

INEZ. I said nothing. Fine. We'll try it your way.

> (She starts to do **FREDDY**'s lips.)

SO LET'S PAINT YOUR LIPS WITH A CARDINAL RED
I HOPED FOR A LADY, BUT IT'S BIMBO INSTEAD
YOUR TASTE IN WOMEN MAKES GOD AND THE VIRGIN
    MOTHER WEEP

FREDDY. You so sure she's a virgin?

INEZ.

HERE YOU GO – SEXY AND CHEAP!

> (She spins **FREDDY** around. This time he is delighted. We cut over to **WES** and **PATRICK**, who are working on the outfit.)

WES. Whaddya think?

(He holds up the outfit in progress. **PATRICK** *laughs.)*

PATRICK. Original.

*(We see **WES** coming alive with joy while he works.)*

You know – this is the first time I've seen you look happy all night.

WES. The past six months all it's been is, *"What's the brand?" Marketing slogans, loans, real estate* – I forgot how good it feels to actually create something.

(Epiphany. He holds up the roll of tape like it's the holy grail.)

This cheap roll of duct tape is giving me life!

*(**BUDDY** calls out to them:)*

BUDDY. You guys almost done?

FREDDY. Done yes. But what is the look we are going for Mama?

INEZ.
    A CLOWN IN A GOWN OR A TWO-DOLLAR WHORE

FREDDY, WES & PATRICK.
    A WHORE!

INEZ.
    WHY WEAR LESS MAKEUP?

INEZ & FREDDY.
    YOU CAN ALWAYS USE MORE!

INEZ.	**FREDDY**.
WASTING MY FAVORITE	**FREDDY**.
ROUGE –	WASTING MY FAVORITE
	ROUGE
ON MY FAVORITE SON!	ON YOUR FAVORITE SON!
AND NOW YOU LOOK –	
	COMPLETELY OVERDONE

WES.	
THIS DRESS...	**PATRICK**.
	COMPLETELY OVERDONE

INEZ, FREDDY, WES & PATRICK.
   COMPLETELY OVERDONE

BUDDY. Hurry up 'cause you've got five minutes.

FREDDY. I can't even tuck in five minutes!

INEZ. Come on Freddy, I'll help you.

FREDDY. Don't help me with *that*!

> *(Song ends.* **INEZ** *tries to put more makeup on* **FREDDY***, but he pushes her hand away.)*

Enough. Where's my dress?

WES. This is the ugliest thing I've ever made.

> *(He gestures to his magnificent dress.* **DALE** *comes over.)*

DALE. Hey Freddy. I know it's not a lot, but I wanted to give you my necklace. It's the only nice thing I own –

> *(He tries to hand* **FREDDY** *his necklace, but* **FREDDY** *is so preoccupied with* **WES***' fabulous dress that he doesn't notice.)*

FREDDY. Oh my god. It's perfect!! I LOVE IT.

> *(He shouts with joy and hugs* **WES***.)*

I'm gonna try it on RIGHT now.

> *(He starts to take off his pants.* **INEZ** *sees someone in the audience staring at him and gasps.)*

INEZ. EH! STOP LOOKING AT MY SLUTTY SON! Freddy –

> *(She grabs her son's ear and drags him to the bathroom, chewing him out under her breath in Spanish. He protests: "Somebody help me! I'm being kidnapped.")*

WES. I love them.

PATRICK. So. You're really talented.

> *(**WES** does a half twirl, bashful.)*

WES. Thanks... I just can't believe I made that hideous dress and no one will get to see it.

PATRICK. What do you mean? We're all gonna see it.

WES. That doesn't count. There's no photos or video. Ugh if I could gram it I'd get at LEAST six thousand likes.

PATRICK. Likes?

WES. I have a *following*.

PATRICK. *(Confused, then excited.)* A following... Are you *famous* or something?

WES. No. Well... / yeah! Exactly. Kind of?

PATRICK. You've been in like. Magazines / and –

WES. *Teen Vogue, W, Vanity Fair*. / No big deal.

PATRICK. Well, I'm sure we're not as cool as your "following" but – think of how much joy you're going to bring to the people here. That's *real*.

(**WES** *laughs at the notion of "real."*)

WES. Who gives a fuck about real? I want content. I want realities that are worth my time. I learned that from reality TV. It's scripted. It's something you perform. And if enough people see it. Then it's real.

PATRICK. So that's what the future's like?

WES. Pretty much. Closets full of high-fashion. All your friends are high-brow.

[MUSIC NO. 08 "THE FUTURE IS GREAT!"]

The highlight of your night is browsing the high-speed web in your high-rise condo. You find out your stock's at an all-time low, but you're too high to care.

(**PATRICK** *laughs, confused, skeptical.*)

You don't seem convinced.

THE FUTURE IS BRIGHT,
FABULOUS, AND CAREFREE.
THE GAYS RUN HALF OF HOLLYWOOD,
AND HOLD HANDS PUBLICLY.
BULLYING'S NOT HALF AS BAD
AS KIDS WOULD LIKE TO CLAIM,
BESIDES, IT GIVES THEM SOMETHING TO VLOG ABOUT
ON THEIR QUEST FOR INSTANT FAME.

PATRICK. What the hell is a vlog...?

WES.

OH! AND GAY MARRIAGE NOW IS LEGAL
THOUGH IN FOUR YEARS, WHO CAN SAY?
YOU GET DEPRESSED JUST SHOP ONLINE
FOR DISCOUNT GAULTIER!
TRAILER TRASH MAKE MILLIONS OFF REALITY TV.

PATRICK. Is that somehow different from reality?

WES. OH yeah.

AIN'T IT GREAT HOW FAR WE'VE COME
SINCE 1973?

> (*The other bar* **PATRONS** *suddenly pop up as Wes'* **FANTASY BACKUP SINGERS** *in matching costumes – like glamorous, ecstatic muppets.*)

YEAH, THE

WES & FANTASY BACKUP SINGERS.

FUTURE IS GREAT!
THERE, YOU ARE WHAT YOU OWN.
IF I COULD TAKE YOU BACK WITH ME
YOUR MIND WOULD BE BLOWN.

WES.

BEING FABULOUS ALL THE TIME
CAN GET A LITTLE PRICEY...
BUT THE FUTURE IS GREAT! TRUST ME.

PATRICK.	**FANTASY BACKUP SINGERS.**
Sounds sparkly. Like a prize on *The Price is Right*.	HMM...

WES. It is! And the bars put UpStairs to shame!

YOU MEET BLUE-EYED BOYS WITH CHEEKBONES
THAT COULD CUT CLEAR THROUGH STEEL
WHO HIDE IN CORNERS CLUTCHING
OVERPRICED DRINKS LIKE A SHIELD
WHILE THEY PRAY TO BE SEEN,
A LOOK INTO THEIR EYES GIVES YOU THE FREEZE –
IT'S LIKE THEY BOTOX'D THEIR SOULS
OR MAYBE THEY'RE JUST SCARED OF THE DISEASE...

PATRICK. Nothing a little penicillin can't cure.

WES.

SINCE TALKING IS TEDIOUS
NOW IPHONES ARE PREFERRED.
YOU CAN KNOW EVERYTHING ABOUT A BOY
WITHOUT SAYING A WORD.
AND IF IT TURNS OUT THAT HE'S USELESS
WHEN HE GETS DOWN ON HIS KNEES

WES.	**FANTASY BACKUP SINGERS.**
AT LEAST HE'LL GO WHEN YOU CUM	CUM! CUM! CUM! CUM!
AND LEAVE NO UNWANTED MYSTERIES.	CUM! CUM!
YEAH, THE FUTURE IS GREAT!	**PATRICK.** THE FUTURE IS GREAT!
DON'T YOU AGREE?	

WES & FANTASY BACKUP SINGERS.

SEX IS QUICK, CONVENIENT, AND USUALLY FREE.

WES.

SOMETIMES I FEAR I'LL NEVER LEARN HOW TO LOVE...
BUT THE FUTURE IS GREAT...SORT OF.
I NEVER HAD A MENTOR,
I'VE BEEN OUT SINCE I WAS TEN,
THOUGH SOMETIMES I WISH
I'D BEEN BORN DIFFERENT NOW AND THEN –
MAYBE THAT'S THE REASON
I'VE A TALENT FOR DESIGN.

(His facade starts to crack. It's existential turmoil with a smile.)

I'M MY BIGGEST, BEST CREATION
CAN'T YOU TELL I TURNED OUT FINE?

FANTASY BACKUP SINGERS.

FINE!

WES.

BUT I GUESS YOU'RE ALSO LUCKY
LIVING IN THE SEVENTIES.
THERE'S NO NEED FOR WEARING CONDOMS

WES.
> YOU CAN SLUT IT UP GUILT-FREE.
> NOWADAYS WE HAVE FANCY DRUGS
> TO HELP US ALL FORGET...
> HOW THE EIGHTIES CAME
> KILLED ALL YOUR FRIENDS
> YOU JUST DON'T KNOW IT YET.

> BUT, THE FUTURE IS GREAT.
> I CAN'T WAIT TO GET BACK AND TAKE

WES & FANTASY BACKUP SINGERS.
> LITTLE WHITE PILLS FOR EACH PANIC ATTACK.

WES.
> JUST UNDER THE TONGUE, IN TEN SECONDS I'M FREE,
> THEN I DON'T HAVE TO THINK
> ABOUT HOW GREAT LIFE'S S'POSED TO BE.

> *(He sees all of his fears and pain before him,
> then, startled by his vulnerability, he snaps
> back.)*

Wow... Uh / sorry! That was very off-brand for me.

PATRICK. Don't worry. It's cool.

WES. I just started therapy... Five years ago / and –

PATRICK. Oh god. They got you too?

WES. I'm trying to be more mindful. Like it's okayyyy to be ashamed of my *voice* and my credit card debt; *everyone* has back fat.

PATRICK. Back fat?

WES. And maybe I AM just another underpaid FIT grad whose life peaked in ninth grade – that day I wore my kimono to school – *everyone* was gagging –

> *(**PATRICK** is confused – isn't "gagging" bad?)*

Like I was going to do something really important with my life. Not – twenty-SEVEN, and still cutting patterns to just barely afford a rat-infested studio in the anus of Brooklyn... So I came home to New Orleans. My parents own a tiny shop off of Bourbon Street. They sell

Mardi Gras beads, beignets, and alligator heads. Half the shit is from China.

(As if describing a prize on Wheel of Fortune*.)* I live in their attic! Hashtag glamour.

PATRICK. *(Optimistic.)* At least your parents *let* you live with them.

WES. It's humiliating. Everyone I know is blowing up, and *I* am the sad statistic in some think piece about how fucked millenials are. This building's my *last* chance to keep my dream alive. I'm half a million dollars in debt. If this fails...

> *(He imagines headlines: "Tragic suicide, artist's life cut short.")*

PATRICK. If what fails?

> *(***WES** *studies* **PATRICK**, *decides not to reveal the truth about the building.)*

WES. ...Nothing. Never mind.

PATRICK. You're being too hard on yourself. Look at me. I'm a total failure. My life's not so bad.

WES. What else do I have to offer? I'm not *masc*, I don't have a six pack, or a stock portfolio.

PATRICK. You just made a dress out of *nothing*!

WES. One dress doesn't make a difference. I want to be somebody. I want to be remembered. I want to be...

> *(Beat.* **PATRICK** *is thrown off by* **WES**'*admission.)*

PATRICK. *Loved?*... That's so old hat. Are you sure you're not from the *past*?

WES. I know. In addition to being average, I'm a basic bitch. Just hand me a pumpkin spice latte and get it over with.

> *(***BUDDY** *steps in and grabs* **PATRICK** *from behind.)*

BUDDY. You and your girlfriend having fun?

WES. So he's just gon' pop up *every* time?

PATRICK. Get off of me –

BUDDY. What? You don't want this anymore? Used to be you couldn't get enough.

> (**WES** *sticks his finger down his throat and pretends to throw up, makes a retching noise.*)

I know you think I'm the punchline to some hilarious joke. But fifteen years ago, every one of my shows sold out. I had execs from Columbia, Atlantic, Stax, flying in to see me play. But I was like you – reckless, holding hands and flirting with boys in public – I thought I was being brave. A trailblazer.

> (*He smiles/chuckles nostalgically.*)

Before I knew it they dropped me, and my career was over. But you don't need to make the same mistake I did. Clean up, get a job, a family. You can buy boys like that any time you want. Say – what's he charging nowadays?

> (**WES**' *face cracks.*)

WES. You were hustling me this whole time?? / I just told you all this vulnerable stuff about myself, like I let you stare into the gaping abyss of my soul and – This is EXTREMELY triggering –

PATRICK. This is different. I wasn't –

BUDDY. Oh please. We all saw you. *"Buy me a drink!"* / Wink wink.

HENRI. Buddy – why you always gotta run your mouth?

BUDDY.	**DALE**.
What? I did him a favor?	Hey Henri! Why doesn't Patrick get a strike?

HENRI. I've given so many strikes today I've lost count.

WES. I'm such an idiot! I thought you actually –

PATRICK. I did. I do! It doesn't change anything.

WES. It changes everything! I can't be emotionally involved with someone who has sex professionally.

WILLIE. *(Triumphant.)* I had this same conversation with Cary Grant!

PATRICK. This isn't who I am. It's what I do to get by.

WES. You know what? You're right. Let's keep everything transactional. And since you did such a good job humoring me, why don't you take my jacket you love so much –

*(He hangs the jacket on **PATRICK**.)*

Think of it as a tip.

PATRICK. What gives you the right to judge me?

WES. I'm not judging you, I just have resting judgmental face.

PATRICK. Nothing bad has ever happened to you. *Everything* / is so easy –

WES. Not everything –

PATRICK. What – you don't like living with your parents? I'll probably never see *my* parents again.

[MUSIC NO. 09 "WALTZ"]

Try being on your own since you were fourteen. Could you do that? Without your money and someone holding your hand and stroking your ego every step of the way? You get to worry about whether or not you're special. I had to stop thinking that way a long time ago.

*(As **PATRICK** sings, the whole atmosphere of the bar becomes introspective and dreamlike as the lighting shifts us into fantasy. Though unaware of each other, some of the other **PATRONS** sing, move along to the waltz, implying a shared experience of trauma and self-discovery.)*

ONCE WHEN I WAS YOUNG
IT SOUNDS CLICHÉ
I DREAMED I'D BUY A ROCKET SHIP
AND SOAR UP TO THE STARS SOMEDAY
FLY TO GALAXIES FAR AWAY.

I GREW UP IN A TOWN – SMALL
ABOUT THREE HOURS FROM HERE

PATRICK.

A PLACE WHERE PEOPLE LOOK AND THINK THE SAME
AND ASTRONAUTS DO NOT APPEAR...OKAY!
I'LL FIND A NEW GAME TO PLAY

TERROR AND BLISS
ON THOSE LAZY AFTERNOONS WHEN I LEARNED HOW TO
    KISS

PATRICK, DALE, HENRI, WILLIE, BUDDY & RICHARD.

AND HE MADE ME UNDERSTAND
WHAT MY BODY WAS FOR

PATRICK.

"AND WE'LL HAVE LOTS OF FUN," HE SAID,
"BUT YOU CAN'T TELL ANYONE."

OUR GAME CAME TO AN END
HIS FATHER SENT HIM AWAY
WITH A PLAN:
"FRY THE FAIRY OUT OF HIM AND HE'LL
COME BACK A MAN MORE OR LESS"
THE DOCTOR GUARANTEED SUCCESS.

BUT TO EVERYONE'S SURPRISE
TOM NEVER SPOKE AGAIN – HE JUST STARES AT THE
    WALL
WHEN OUR FAM'LY GATHERS 'ROUND ON HOLIDAYS
THEY ALL PRETEND IT'S OKAY
"HE'S BETTER OFF THIS WAY."

BUT I'D RATHER DIE
THAN END UP LIKE HIM:
DULL AND DEAD IN THE EYES

PATRICK, DALE, HENRI, WILLIE, BUDDY & RICHARD.

AND IT WAS ONLY A MATTER OF TIME
BEFORE THEY'D TRY TO FIX ME THE SAME WAY.

PATRICK.

PACKED UP MY LIFE IN ONE BAG
AND I HAVEN'T BEEN BACK.

> *(The bar starts to fade away as he retreats
> into his mind.)*

BEING A LITTLE TOO FREE
IS NOT ALWAYS GLAM'ROUS
BUT YOU LEARN HOW TO SURVIVE

LIFE PRESSES ON, YOU CREATE LITTLE STORIES
TO KEEP YOUR HEART ALIVE
WHY GET TOO HUNG UP ON THE PAST
WHEN YOU CAN'T HIT REWIND?
HOPE WHEN I LOOK BACK I CAN SMILE
AND SAY IT WAS WORTH IT ALL TO FIND
A LOVE OF MY OWN SOMEDAY
THAT CAN'T BE TAKEN AWAY

> *(The spotlight slowly fades away as light gradually returns to the rest of the bar.)*

AND IF ONE DAY I HAVE THE MONEY
A ROCKET SHIP'S NOT WHAT I'LL BUY
'CAUSE I KNOW BETTER NOW
THERE'S NO MORE STARS LEFT IN THE SKY
JUST ENDLESS NIGHT.

> *(**WES** is deeply moved by **PATRICK**'s story. He embraces **PATRICK**, who is very surprised.)*

What are you doing?

WES. I don't know...

> *(They have a moment. **PATRICK** grabs **WES** and finally kisses him for real. It's true and beautiful and kinda hot.)*

Oh.

> *(**WILLIE** writhes with delight.)*

WILLIE. *Oh!* And just when I thought romance was dead –
HELLO YOUNG LOVERRRRRRRRS
Bravo!

> *(He puts his arm around **WES** and **PATRICK**.)*

I think you two have reminded us *all* something very important today.

RICHARD. The power of friendship, compassion, love!

*(**WILLIE** screams:)*

WILLIE. NO!!!!

(Abruptly switches to a lighter tone.) Much more important than any of that – You remind me of my youth.

HENRI. Uh-oh, here we go.

> *(As **WILLIE** launches into his speech, some of the other **PATRONS** mouth along – they've heard it so many times they've got their favorite parts memorized. **WILLIE** works the room as if delivering a grandiose aria.)*

WILLIE. All you kids are spoiled. Nowadays you can't walk into a bathroom without ten guys following you into your stall, but once upon a time, things were not so simple. There was no cruising on the breadlines! Why, in my early twenties I had to intercept more coded messages than the allied forces...

> *(He intercepts a code from an audience member, flirts back.)*

But I was hungry for love, and I certainly found it. Painters, poets, diplomats, sailors galore, even a sword swallower. I had them all. They of course fell deeply in love with me. How could they not?

> *(He gives an audience member a death stare, like, "I dare you to tell me I'm not stunning." He smiles and goes back to the aria.)*

It's an undisputed fact I had the best legs in all New Orleans – for a man *or* a woman, Mr. Balanchine told me himself when I auditioned for the Ballet Russes de Monte Carlo in 19–

> *(He waves his hands in a **PATRON**'s face to distract them.)*

Now mind you I'm no dancer –

> *(He does an outrageous, spectacular dance that culminates with him throwing his leg onto the piano.)*

But he was ready to take me on my silhouette alone, except for that nasty prima ballerina, Danilova. Oh, she was a fright, and jealous too. How I would've loved to tweeze every wayward hair off her boorish Russian face, but who'd have known where to begin?

> *(He plucks phantom hairs off an audience member's face. Eventually he snaps out of his trance, runs to center stage, and thrusts his arms into the air.)*

That's all!

> *(He bows, soaking up the adoration and rapturous applause.)*

WES. What does any of that have to do with us?

WILLIE. Huh?! Oh...

> *(He looks into* **WES** *and* **PATRICK***; he sees potential.)*

I'm an old queen, but you're still a fetus.

> *(Beat. Then, with love:)*

So keep growing.

> *(Suddenly the lights shift as the piano roars to life for* **FREDDY***'s drag number.)*

And go to as many drag shows as humanly possible!

> *(Lights shift.* **WILLIE** *emcees excitedly.)*

Ladies and gentlemen, please welcome the filthiest piece of swamp trash to ever crawl out the bayou, Miss AURORA WHOREALIS!

[MUSIC NO. 10 "SEX ON LEGS"]

> *(Suddenly* **PATRICK** *sees* **FREDDY** *walk onstage wearing a nun's habit. He carries a ruler, which he uses to slap the other people in the bar suggestively. The crowd goes wild.)*

WES. WERRRRRRRRK!!!!

*(**PATRICK** grabs **WES** and they run toward the makeshift stage, over which a small disco ball now hangs. **FREDDY** takes a shot, then sings.)*

FREDDY.

I WAS HOOKED FROM THE START.
YOU'RE LIKE A WORK OF ART,
I'M A BOX WITHOUT A PRIZE
BUT ONE OF THESE DAYS
I'M GONNA STEAL YOU AWAY
AND ALL THAT THAT IMPLIES...
'CAUSE YOU'RE SEX ON LEGS
I'M OH SO SHY
ONE LOOK AND I TURN
INTO A FIFTIES HOUSEWIFE
IN MY MIND I'M SCREAMING OUT YOUR NAME.
BUT IN LIFE I GOT NO GAME.

*(**FREDDY** rips off the nun's habit to reveal Wes' outrageous couture dress made out of the knick-knacks taken from the bar.)*

ALL.

SCREAMING OUT YOUR NAME, SCREAMING OUT YOUR NAME, SCREAMING OUT YOUR NAME!

FREDDY.

BUT IN LIFE I GOT NO GAME.

ALL.

SCREAMING OUT YOUR NAME, SCREAMING OUT YOUR NAME, SCREAMING OUT YOUR NAME!

WILLIE.	**FREDDY.**
BUT IN LIFE SHE'S GOT NO GAME.	I SMILE

FREDDY.

AND SAY HI
THEN SLOWLY DIE INSIDE
THE EFFECT IS RATHER STRANGE
LIKE A SENSE-DEPRIVED FLY
I'VE BEEN BUZZING 'ROUND BLIND
WON'T YOU DROP ME A CRUMB FOR A CHANGE?

(Someone hands him a dollar. He licks their face.)

FREDDY.
'CAUSE YOU'RE SEX ON
    LEGS
I'M OH SO SHY
ONE LOOK AND I TURN
INTO A FIFTIES HOUSEWIFE
IN MY MIND I'M SCREAMING
    OUT YOUR NAME

OTHERS.
OOO-OOO
FIFTIES HOUSEWIFE

WILLIE.
SCREAMING OUT YOUR
    NAME.

HOW'D I FALL SO HARD?
I CAN'T EVEN RECALL
OTHER THAN YOUR BOD
YOU DON'T IMPRESS ME AT
    ALL
WON'T LOOK YOU IN THE
    EYES
WAIT BY THE PHONE ALL
    NIGHT
I'LL NEVER GAWK AGAIN...
OOO

OTHERS.
OOO OOO
NEVER AGAIN!

NEVER AGAIN!
BUT HOW LONG COULD I
    LAST
WHEN YOUR GOD-GIVEN
    ASS
HAS GOT ITS
OWN GRAVITATIONAL
    SUCK?
IN MY PERSONAL HELL
IF I HAD A SOUL TO SELL
I WOULD TRADE IT IN FOR
    JUST ONE

OHH!!

(**FREDDY** *shakes his breasts, which explode with confetti right at the climax of the song as* **INEZ** *chucks a bucket of glitter into the air. It rains down as everyone dances and sings.* **HENRI** *screams.*)

FREDDY.
'CAUSE YOU'RE
OTHERS.
SEX

(**HENRI** *joins.*)

ALL.
ON LEGS
I'M OH SO SHY
FREDDY.
ONE LOOK AND I TURN
INTO A
ALL.
FIFTIES HOUSEWIFE
FREDDY.
IN MY MIND I'M
ALL.
SCREAMING OUT
FREDDY.
YOUR NAME
WES, BUDDY, DALE, WILLIE, RICHARD & COP.
NAME
PATRICK, INEZ & HENRI.
NAME
FREDDY.
BUT IN LIFE I GOT NO

FREDDY.	**OTHERS.**
GAME.	SCREAMING

(**FREDDY** *passes around the charity jar from before. Everyone reaches into their pockets to find money to place in it, so that by the time the song is finished the jar is once again full.*

DALE *tries to use this opportunity to solicit the*
PATRONS, *but he gets brushed off repeatedly.*
We see his frustration building.)

OTHERS.
OUT YOUR NAME, SCREAMING OUT YOUR NAME,
SCREAMING OUT YOUR

OTHERS.	**FREDDY.**
NAME!	BUT IN LIFE

FREDDY.
I'VE GOT NO

FREDDY.	**OTHERS.**
GAME.	SCREAMING

OTHERS.
OUT YOUR NAME, SCREAMING OUT YOUR NAME,
SCREAMING OUT YOUR NAME!

FREDDY.	**OTHERS.**
BUT IN LIFE	NAME!

FREDDY.	**INEZ, HENRI, WILLIE, PATRICK & DALE.**	**BUDDY, WES & RICHARD.**
I GOT NO –		
	SEX ON LEGS	SCREAMING OUT YOUR NAME.
	I'M OH SO SHY.	SCREAMING OUT YOUR NAME.
		SCREAMING OUT YOUR
BUT IN LIFE I GOT NO		NAME.
GAME	IN MY MIND I'M	SCREAMING OUT YOUR NAME.
	SCREAMING OUT YOUR NAME.	SCREAMING OUT YOUR NAME.
		SCREAMING OUT YOUR
BUT IN LIFE I GOT NO		NAME.

FREDDY.	INEZ, HENRI, WILLIE, PATRICK & DALE.	BUDDY, WES & RICHARD.
	SEX ON LEGS I'M OH SO SHY.	SCREAMING OUT YOUR NAME. SCREAMING OUT YOUR NAME. SCREAMING OUT
BUT IN LIFE I GOT NO GAME	IN MY MIND I'M SCREAMING OUT YOUR NAME.	YOUR NAME. SCREAMING OUT YOUR NAME. SCREAMING OUT YOUR NAME. SCREAMING OUT YOUR
BUT IN LIFE I GOT NO GAME		NAME.

(FREDDY raises the now-full money jar above his head triumphantly.)

HENRI. You're killing me. Every week with this confetti and glitter.

FREDDY. Sparkly things make people spend money.

(He quickly hands RICHARD the jar.)

RICHARD. Look how much we raised!

(People applaud. INEZ shouts, "WEPA!")

WES. Freddy!

WILLIE. Careful now! This is the legendary Miss Aurora Whorealis. Address her properly.

WES. Aurora, you are a sickening fierce bitch!

(People gasp.)

You were giving me cunt for days.

(Even louder gasps.)

INEZ. *(Outraged.)* What the hell kind of compliment is that??

WES. Sorry – I'm just – feeling feelings? I had no budget, no real fabric, and put –

> *(Gestures to his dress.)*

Whatever-this-is together in twenty minutes, but your *performance* – It was so...subversive, but also camp, and like *political*.

> *(He gasps, then, deadpan:)*

But you made it fashion.

FREDDY. Yeah okay sure, but do you also make TIARAS?

WES. *(Giddy.)* I'd like to try.

FREDDY. AH! I can't wait for you to make me a Whole. New. Wardrobe!

> *(He suddenly gets woozy, gags. He tries to laugh it off.)*

And on that note! I think my concussion is kicking in. Excuse me. I'm going to be sick!

> *(He runs toward the restroom, not seeing* **DALE***, who runs up to him.)*

DALE. Hey Aurora. That was amazing, you get better and better every time. I loved the part when you –

> **(FREDDY** *collides with* **DALE***, spilling the beer down his dress.)*

FREDDY. My dress / that was couture. You idiot – I've never owned something this nice –

DALE. Oh no. Oh god. I'm so sorry. I didn't mean to –

[MUSIC NO. 11 "BETTER THAN SILENCE"]

FREDDY. Just get out of my way!

> *(He groans, swats* **DALE** *away, and keeps running.)*

INEZ. *(To* **DALE***, apologetically.)* Sorry – nothing personal.

*(She chases after **FREDDY**.)*

DALE. Don't worry. It never is.
IT'S SO FUN BEIN' INVISIBLE
YOU DON'T HAVE TO WORRY ABOUT
WHAT TO WEAR OR WHERE YOU'RE GOIN'
BECAUSE NOBODY CARES

I TRIED TO GIVE FREDDY MY NECKLACE
THE ONE NICE THING I OWN
I PICK GUM OFF THE BOTTOM OF BARSTOOLS
TO SHOW HENRI HOW MUCH I'VE GROWN
TO CONTRIBUTE, I SET UP THE CHAIRS
AND WATCH HOW YOU SQUANDER YOUR PRAYERS
BUT IT'S BETTER THAN SILENCE.
IT'S BETTER THAN SILENCE.

YOU HEAR THINGS, WHEN YOU'RE INVISIBLE
PEOPLE SPEAK THEIR MINDS LIKE YOU CAN'T HEAR
AS IF THEIR WHISPERS AREN'T PAINFULLY CLEAR

> *(He proceeds to work the room, trying to hustle a bunch of **PATRONS** in succession.)*

HELLO. CAN YOU HELP ME?
I'M TRYIN' TO GET BACK ON MY FEET.
AND IT'S TWENTY A NIGHT FOR A HOTEL;
A COUPLE OF DRINKS AND PLACE TO SLEEP.
CAN YOU HEAR ME? I CAN HELP YOU.
I CAN BE A SLUT; I CAN BE DISCREET
I PROMISE I'M NOT GONNA HURT YOU,
I'LL DO ANYTHING FOR PRETTY CHEAP.

AND I GET: NOTHING. SILENCE.
OR, "NOT TODAY." OR, "WHAT DO I LOOK LIKE – A
    CHARITY?"
"FREAAAAK," "HAHAHA," "GET OUT OF MY HOUSE!"
"WITH THAT FACE YOU OUGHTA PAY *ME*."
I DON'T ASK FOR MUCH, OR NEED TO BE ADORED
BUT HOW DO YOU GET USED TO BEING IGNORED?

THERE COMES A POINT
WHEN YOU'RE INVISIBLE

WHEN YOU'LL SCREAM "FIRE!!"
IN A CROWDED THEATER
TO SEE IF ANYONE CAN HEAR.
'CAUSE IT'S BETTER THAN SILENCE.
'CAUSE IT'S BETTER THAN SILENCE.

> *(His song goes unheard by everyone in the bar. They're too busy being entertained by* **WILLIE**.*)*

WILLIE. I gave my debut performance in the Metropolitan Opera only a couple hours after being stabbed in the neck. Did I complain??

> *(***WES*** runs back to* ***PATRICK***, *raising his glass in the air.)*

WES. I LOVE THIS BUSTED ASS BAR!

PATRICK. It's not so bad right?

WES. It's a shame I um...

> *(He quietly lets* **PATRICK** *in on a secret, knowing it's not going to go well:)*

It's getting torn down next week.

PATRICK. *(Smiling.)* What are you talking about?

WES. I bought the bar – *Surprise!*

> *(Doesn't go well. He recalibrates.)*

It's going to be my flagship store.

PATRICK. Wait. You're serious? This place is sacred. We need it. You can't tear it down. Where's your sense of community?

WES. There will be a community! An even better one – with artists, and influencers. Patent leather walls. A glass floor. Neon sculptures.

PATRICK. The UpStairs welcomed me with open arms. Buddy lent me money. Richard let me sleep at his place. Do you know how many dinners Henri has hosted here? How many plays Willie has starred in. Every single piece of glitter in here, embedded in the floor, comes from one of Freddy's performances. Why would you want to destroy that?

WES. Because the world has gone insane – I have to look out for myself. If I'm going to make anything better, first I need influence, I need a *brand*, an empire –

PATRICK. I *hate* your STUPID fucking brand!

WES. Look. I get it. I do. But in my world, gay bars have no reason to exist. The drinks are overpriced and watered down, we don't need them for sex, we certainly don't need them for community – they're not even *for* us anymore anyway. They stay in business by hosting bachelorette parties and playing Top-40 hits. There's no great culture there worth saving. All of *this* has been on life support for decades, I'm just the one with the courage to pull the plug.

PATRICK. No one in that world will ever have your back, the way we have each other's here. And what, you just wanna be the amusing faggot at their table?

WES. If the table's at a three-star Michelin restaurant, sure.

PATRICK. Why is it *all* about money to you?

WES. What else would it be about? When rich people buy my clothing, that says I have status. That status means cops can't just arrest me for no reason; I can't be fired from my job if I'm the CEO. We are going to be a billion-dollar industry. And when you have that kind of power, you can buy respect.

PATRICK. But you can't buy a home.

　　　　(Beat.)

WES. I promise you, you're going to thank me one day. I am your generation's wildest dreams. I am what it looks like when you finally let go of your trauma.

PATRICK. If that's true I'd rather keep it then.

　　　　(He storms off. **INEZ** *brings* **WES** *a drink and grabs him by the arm maternally.)*

INEZ. You know, once upon a time I used to be the one sewing my son's outfits? I see I have competition!

　　　　*(***WES*** *stutters apologetically.)*

Don't worry. Thank you for helping Freddy. I don't believe we've officially met. I'm Inez.

WES. Wes.

INEZ. You know sometimes I talk to these men. They confide in me, I give them advice. You can talk to me too. You have a thing for Patrick?

(She nudges **WES** *like "hubba hubba.")*

WES. I just met him! ...He's *okay*.

INEZ. We are talking only two seconds and already you are lying.

WES. When I woke up today, falling for a hustler was not what I imagined for myself. None of this was.

INEZ. ...Believe it or not, I didn't think when I moved here that my son would be wearing dresses and that I would be in this room sometimes three nights a week.

[MUSIC NO. 12 "THE MOST IMPORTANT THING"]

That was not my dream. Doing my son's nails? Throwing glitter in the air? No. It's fun *now*, but NO.

BACK IN PUERTO RICO
I HELPED THE PAGEANT QUEENS
STITCH AND SEW DRESSES
I SAVED A LITTLE MONEY
TO MOVE HERE AND MAKE MY OWN FAMILY
BUY THE BIG PRETTY HOUSE THAT YOU SEE ON T.V.

SO WHAT THE HELL IS WITH THIS PERMANENT SMELL?
THE CARPET'S STAINED, THE ROOM'S TOO SMALL
MY HUSBAND SAID THE RENT IS CHEAP,
I HEAR GUNSHOTS AS WE SLEEP
AND THINK GOD THIS WAS NOT MY DREAM AT ALL.

LIFE DIDN'T GO AS PLANNED, BUT I LEARNED TO PLAY
    ALONG
AND MAYBE THIS HAD TO HAPPEN TO TEACH ME HOW TO
    BE STRONG
WHO KNOWS WHAT THE FUTURE BRINGS? ONLY GOD
    ABOVE.

INEZ.

YOU CAN GIVE UP ON SO MANY THINGS, BUT YOU CAN'T
GIVE UP ON LOVE.
¿Entiendes?

WES. Sorry, I took French.

*(**INEZ** rolls her eyes.)*

INEZ.

AS FREDDY GREW UP,
I NOTICED SOMETHING STRANGE:
MY LIPSTICKS AND POWDERS WOULD SOMETIMES BE
REARRANGED
WHEN MY HUSBAND FOUND OUT OUR SON WAS THAT
WAY
HE TURNED OFF HIS LOVE, AND JUST LEFT US ONE DAY

NOW I'M ALONE, IN A CITY NOT MY OWN
SINGLE MOTHER, UNEMPLOYED...
AND WHILE I LOOK FOR A CAREER MY SON ENDS UP HERE
MAKING FRIENDS WITH PEOPLE I WAS TAUGHT TO AVOID.

INEZ.

LIFE DIDN'T GO AS PLANNED	**HENRI, FREDDY, WES, WILLIE & RICHARD.**
BUT I LEARNED TO PLAY ALONG	LEARN TO PLAY ALONG.
AND MAYBE THIS HAD TO HAPPEN	

INEZ, HENRI, FREDDY, WES, WILLIE & RICHARD.

TO TEACH ME HOW TO BE STRONG.
WHO KNOWS WHAT THE FUTURE BRINGS?
ONLY GOD ABOVE.
YOU CAN GIVE UP ON SO MANY THINGS
BUT YOU CAN'T GIVE UP ON LOVE.

INEZ.

SOMETIMES YOU WANT TO RUN AWAY BUT LOVE'S TOO
STRONG
THE DISAPPOINTMENT DOESN'T LAST FOR VERY LONG

AND WHO'S TO SAY WHAT'S REALLY RIGHT AND WHAT IS
    WRONG?
YOU DECIDE FOR YOURSELF.
THIS ISN'T WHAT I WOULD HAVE CHOSE BUT IT'S OKAY
AND IF MY FRIENDS COULD SEE ME NOW HERE'S WHAT
    I'D SAY:
"I THINK GAY MEN ARE MORE FUN ANYWAY..."
PEOPLE CAN BE CRUEL
THIS LIFE IS NOT EASY
BUT IF YOUR SON IS A DRAG QUEEN
AT LEAST SEWING COMES IN HANDY
SO I LEARNED HOW TO SEE A NEW POINT OF VIEW
ON LOVE THAT'S THE MOST IMPORTANT THING YOU CAN
    DO.

WES. I can't imagine going through all that. You're like some fantasy mother.

INEZ. I am *just* a mother, and I love my son. To come here tonight, that took some courage, but you are already here. The hard part is over. Look around the room – how many of them would trade their left huevo for a chance at what you and that boy could have?

> (**PATRICK** *exits the bathroom.*)

There he is now! Well? What are you waiting for? Go.

WES. I don't think –

INEZ. GO!

> (*She pushes* **WES** *forward. He walks over to* **PATRICK** *sheepishly. He is at once still upset and relieved to see him.*)

WES. Do you actually hate my brand?!

> (*He prepares to say something emotionally true, then:*)

Ugh! Wait. That came out wrong.

PATRICK. I don't think I like *you*.

WES. Great. I don't like me either.

PATRICK. So make something new! Isn't that your job?

WES. I make outfits. I just make people *look* better.

PATRICK. I should go. You're better off without me anyway.

(*He starts to leave.* **WES** *grabs him.*)

WES. What are you talking about?

PATRICK. I'll never be like you. You have all this talent and drive and potential to do incredible things and I'm here. This is my life.

WES. So *write* about it. There's gotta be a book deal there.

PATRICK. You're impossible.

WES. (*Frustrated.*) I know. Dammit. WHY IS THIS SO HARD? Hold on.

(*He closes his eyes and starts whispering to himself and making strange sounds while doing ridiculous over-the-top interpretive dancey things with his hands.*)

PATRICK. Uh. What are you doing?

[MUSIC NO. 13 "A CRAZY INTRO"]

WES. Accessing my emotions!
I'VE SPENT HALF THE NIGHT
CONFUSED AND FRIGHTENED,
LIKE A BASKET CASE
WOND'RING HOW THE HELL
I EVER ENDED UP HERE IN THE FIRST PLACE
GOT SO CAUGHT UP IN TRYING TO FIND
A REASON TO RUN AWAY.
IT NEVER CROSSED MY MIND I'D WANNA STAY.

(*He grabs a microphone and jumps on the piano like a chanteuse.*)

BUT YOU GAVE ME A REASON TO
CHILL THE FUCK OUT.
IT'S TRUE I HATE MYSELF,
BUT I'D HATE MYSELF MORE IF YOU WEREN'T AROUND.
I'D BERATE MYSELF, EMOTION'LLY CASTRATE MYSELF
I'D SELF-MEDICATE, HYPERVENTILATE, AND EVENTU'LLY
    BREAK DOWN.

WHILE YOU'RE PEACEFULLY SLEEPIN', I'LL BE STUCK
WEEPIN'
IN MY PADDED CELL. 'CAUSE I'M AN IMPOSSIBLE MESS
THAT NO ONE COULD POSSIBLY FIX AS WELL AS YOU.

PATRICK. This is emotional blackmail.

WES. Uh-huh. Is it working?

PATRICK. No! ...Kind of?

*(**WES** rolls up his sleeves.)*

WES. Great! Well I'm just getting started.

SO GIVE ME ANOTHER CHANCE TO RUIN YOUR LIFE!
I'M A WORK IN PROGRESS BUT I PROMISE I'LL TRY TO

[MUSIC NO. 13A "A CRAZY NOTION"]

*(He switches tactics, to something more
upbeat and playful. He twirls, bounces
around, etc.)*

LOVE MYSELF UNCONDITIONALLY,
BE A PERSON NOT A PERSONALITY

PATRICK.

THAT SOUNDS PROMISING

WES.

WELL, SELF-AWARENESS *IS* MY NEW THANG
'CAUSE I'M A –

OTHERS.

SHADY BITCH

WES. Okay!

(He shoots everyone an insulted look!)

ONCE AND A WHILE
BUT I PROMISE NOT TO READ YOU
FOR YOUR RETRO STYLE.

PATRICK.

YOU'RE ACTING ALL...ROMANTIC.
DID YOU HIT YOUR HEAD?

WES.

IT'S A CRAZY NOTION –
I'M NOT GOOD WITH EMOTION,

WES.

> BUT TONIGHT THE RULES HAVE ALL BEEN SHATTERED
> AND NOW IRONY'S JUST A CRUTCH
> I DON'T MISS MY OLD LIFE THAT MUCH.
> WHEN I'M BESIDE YOU NOTHING ELSE MATTERS
> I FIN'LLY KNOW WHAT THAT FEELS LIKE.

PATRICK. Wes – remember, I've got no money, we have nowhere / to sleep –

WES. We've got each other! Besides, I watched five episodes of *Survivor*. I'm totally prepared to live off the grid.

PATRICK. Oh god.

WES.

> WE'LL HITCH A RIDE IN A ROWBOAT TOGETHER ACROSS
>   THE BAYOU.

PATRICK.

> LIVE IN THE MIDDLE OF NOWHERE – POPULATION OF TWO.

WES.

> AND I'LL GATHER WOOD!

PATRICK.

> I'LL LEARN HOW TO HUNT.

> *(He flexes his muscle with* **HENRI.***)*

WES.

> I'LL TRY HARD TO BE A LITTLE LESS OF A C–

> *(***PATRICK** *playfully covers* **WES***' mouth with his hand.)*

PATRICK.

> WE'LL SLEEP WITH THE WOLVES IN THEIR FOREST DEN.

WES.

> WHEN YOU LOOK UP AT THE SKY YOU'LL SEE THE STARS
>   AGAIN.
> SEE IT ALL AGAIN.

WES & PATRICK.

> IT'S A CRAZY NOTION –
> I'M NOT GOOD WITH EMOTION,
> BUT TONIGHT

WES.

THE RULES HAVE BEEN SHATTERED:

PATRICK.

THE RULES HAVE BEEN SHATTERED!

WES.

I DON'T NEED BITTERNESS ANYMORE.
THAT MADE UP MY

WES & PATRICK.

WHOLE LIFE BEFORE.
WHEN I'M BESIDE YOU NOTHING ELSE MATTERS.
I FIN'LLY
KNOW WHAT THAT FEELS LIKE.

PATRICK.

IF THIS WAS A MOVIE IT'D END LIKE THIS:
SHOT OF A SUNSET, THE LOVERS KISS –

WES.

BUT THIS IS REAL –
AND I FEEL LIKE THE CLAY SPINNING ON A POTTER'S
    WHEEL!

PATRICK.

THOUGH IT WAS NOT LOVE AT FIRST SIGHT –

WES & PATRICK.

IT'S OUR STORY AND THE ENDING'S OURS TO WRITE.

WES.

AND WHO'D HAVE THOUGHT

PATRICK.

WHO'D HAVE THOUGHT

WES.

IT'D TURN OUT THIS WAY?

PATRICK.

IT'D TURN OUT THIS WAY?

WES.

I DON'T UNDERSTAND
    THE CRAZY
THINGS THAT KEEP
    HAPPENING

    PATRICK.

    I DON'T UNDERSTAND
      THE CRAZY

WES.	PATRICK.
TO ME TODAY	THINGS THAT KEEP HAPPENING TO ME TODAY
YOU'RE JUST ANOTHER MAGIC UNEXPLAINED PHENOMENON	MAGIC UNEXPLAINED PHENOMENON
	AND IT'S A
AND IT'S A	CRAZY
CRAZY NOTION.	CRAZY NOTION.

WILLIE. Henri. Am I in the early stages of dementia or are these two boys falling in love?

HENRI. *(Unamused.)* Both.

FREDDY. But in THIS bar??

RICHARD. It's a miracle!

WILLIE. Well what are we going to do about it? My careful eavesdropping has informed me they have nowhere to sleep for the night.

HENRI. Don't look at me.

WILLIE. Oh come on Henri! You've been in love once. How many times did you drag my ass to the *Daughters of Bilitis* just so you could catch a glimpse of –

HENRI. OKAY! That's enough about me!

> *(She looks at* **WES** *and* **PATRICK**, *thinks, sighs, relents.)*

Fine. After I close up tonight, if y'all accidentally find yourselves locked inside, then I'm sure I don't know anything about it... But remember I measure the booze every night before I leave. If I come back and find you guys went all Janis Joplin on this place, you're back out on your ass. Is that understood?

WES & PATRICK. Yes!

> *(***PATRONS*** cheer.* **DALE***'s frustration starts to build.)*

HENRI. Good. There's a cot in the back and I got a wool blanket I can give you.

WILLIE. Henri, I hope you're not talking about that old Hoover blanket? Smells like balls and it ain't been touched since the Depression.

HENRI. It'll get the job done –

WILLIE. If the job is catching syphilis! Honey, I've got a better idea. You see, I had a dream –

HENRI. Oh. Dr. King...

WILLIE. That two star-crossed lovers might one day find themselves in need of a little warmth and opulence, so I casually tossed a pair of fur-lined cashmere capes into the trunk of my car, where they've been languishing ever since. Simply unbutton and voila, it's comforter de luxe by Halston.

(People laugh, cheer.)

FREDDY. SLUMBER PARTY!

*(***DALE*** explodes:)*

DALE. WHAT THE FUCK? How is it Patrick *always* gets a free pass here and not me? You turn a blind eye night after night while he picks up his johns. And I get treated like some kind of freakshow. Is it because he's pretty? Is it because he has that sad wounded puppy dog look in his eyes – *"I was abused."* Tough shit. I've been abused. You don't see me crying about it.

HENRI. Give it a rest, Dale.

DALE. WHY SHOULD I?

(To everyone in the bar.) You preach about acceptance and love, so why can't you accept ME? Why can't you love ME? You all know I'm homeless. You all know I'm suffering. Never ONCE have you offered me a place to stay or a fucking blanket.

BUDDY. It's because you're a mental case! You're a drunk, you have no friends, you sell your ass for five dollars. People know you're a low-life. When they see you walking in here, they think we're all like you.

DALE. Stop putting how much you hate yourself on me.

FREDDY. Baby, calm down.

HENRI. It's not just about you Dale. We gotta think about *all* the people who've got nowhere else to go. I can't afford to lose the shirt off my back tryna reign in your crazy.

BUDDY. It's people like *you* who make me feel ashamed.

DALE. You should be – the way you bent over for that cop. And you know – I think you're the real threat to our community –

WILLIE. Come on, Dale. Let's go take a walk.

DALE. I've got nothing to lose. But you live in constant fear of being discovered. You lie to people you love / every day.

BUDDY. I'm protecting us; some of us have reputations worth / protecting.

DALE. You're just living some fantasy – In fact, why don't we fix that right now. Here – I'll tell 'em myself.

(He goes to the phone behind the bar.)

What's your wife's number?

HENRI. Hey!

*(She grabs the phone away from **DALE**.)*

BUDDY. See that? He's out of control. / And you are finished here!

RICHARD. Buddy – he's just in pain. We can't turn away the most vulnerable among us.

INEZ. You saw what happened to my son out there.

WILLIE. Maybe he's a little bit of a basket case, but who isn't really? I mean look at us? No really. Look!

PATRICK. Dale, you can have the cot, take the blanket – I don't need it.

DALE. I'm not asking for charity. I'm just trying to be *seen*.

BUDDY. Everybody sees you Dale. That's the problem. We should've gotten rid of him months ago.

*(He starts pushing **DALE** toward the door.)*

You are not a part of our community. You are NOT welcome here –

WILLIE. Buddy stop it.

BUDDY. THE ONLY PLACE YOU WILL EVER BELONG IS IN AN ASYLUM.

> *(A fight breaks out.* **DALE** *punches* **BUDDY** *in the face, knocking him to the floor. He starts to kick him when* **HENRI** *intervenes.)*

HENRI. STOP. NO FIGHTING.

> *(***DALE** *spits in her face. Beat.* **HENRI** *is deeply hurt.)*

Get the hell out of my bar.

> *(***DALE** *staggers to the door, takes a look at everyone in the room, humiliated, intoxicated, full of rage.)*

DALE. What do I have to do to make you see me?

> *(He exits.)*

RICHARD. What's gotten into all of you? We are better than this!

HENRI. He *spit* on me.

RICHARD. Jesus tur–

HENRI. Then Jesus can buy my bar and run it himself.

RICHARD. We've got to stick together. *Buddy* –

BUDDY. Oh spare me the guilt trip. I did what I was supposed to do. I manned up. I made sacrifices none of you kids would have the courage to make.

> *(***FREDDY** *gestures to his dress.)*

FREDDY. You think this doesn't take courage? Last time I checked I was the one getting my face kicked in.

BUDDY. Well now we've both got our faces kicked in. Happy??

> *(He gestures to his coming black eye.)*

How am I gonna explain *this*?

PATRICK. Why *don't* you tell them the truth.

BUDDY. And ruin my kids' lives, / destroy my family –

> (**INEZ** *gestures to herself and* **FREDDY**.)

INEZ. It made us stronger!

RICHARD. We're also your family.

WILLIE. Are you in the life or not?

> (**BUDDY**, *struggling, emotional, shakes his head.*)

BUDDY. I'm here aren't I? This is all I have left to look forward to. I wish to God things were different. I –

> (*He is overwhelmed, shakes his head.*)

Sorry. I'll just get outta your way.

> (*He grabs his things and goes to leave.* **WILLIE** *starts to sing the bar's theme song, which stops* **BUDDY** *in his tracks.*)

[MUSIC NO. 14 "THEME SONG"]

WILLIE.

IF THE HEAVENS ABOVE YOU
SHOULD COME CRASHING DOWN
LIKE A HOUSE OF CARDS THAT THE WIND KNOCKS
SO EAS'LY TO THE GROUND

> (**FREDDY** *begins to sing. The song begins to heal the room.*)

WILLIE & FREDDY.

I'LL BE RIGHT

FREDDY.

THERE BESIDE YOU, 'TIL THE VERY END.

WILLIE & FREDDY.

TO PICK THE PIECES UP AND HELP YOU BUILD IT BACK
'TIL IT'S

WILLIE, FREDDY & RICHARD.

SKY-HIGH AGAIN.

WILLIE.

AND THE NIGHTS WE BRAVED TOGETHER
LIVE ON INSIDE OUR HEARTS.

WE'VE GOT AN IRON BOND NO HATE COULD BREAK
  APART.

*(He gestures to **BUDDY** to join them again at
the piano.)*

NOW AND FOREVER, COME WHATEVER, YOU AND I.

*(**BUDDY** takes over at the piano again.)*

BUDDY.
  YES, THIS LIFE'S A ROLLER COASTER;

INEZ.
  YOU BLINK AND IT'S DONE.

HENRI.
  AND IT'S HARD TO MAKE THE FLEETING MOMENTS COUNT
  WHEN YOU'RE LIVING –

ALL.
  UNDER THE GUN.

WILLIE.
  BUT I SWEAR

PATRICK.
  I SWEAR

WILLIE.
  I'VE SEEN THE FUTURE

PATRICK.
  I'VE SEEN THE FUTURE

*(They all turn to **WES**.)*

FREDDY, PATRICK & WILLIE.
  SHINING

PATRICK, WILLIE, HENRI, FREDDY & INEZ.
  THROUGH THE DEBRIS

WILLIE.
  AND THOUGH WE'VE KNOWN DESPAIR,

PATRICK & RICHARD.
  THOUGH WE'VE KNOWN DESPAIR

WILLIE.
  WE'RE STILL STANDING THERE

HENRI, PATRICK & RICHARD.
> WE'RE STILL STANDING THERE

HENRI, PATRICK, RICHARD, BUDDY & WILLIE.
> UNBROKEN AND FREE.

>> (**PATRICK** *extends his hand toward* **WES,**
>> *inviting him to join their circle around the*
>> *piano; their community.*)

WILLIE.

AND	**BUDDY.**	
THE	THE	**PATRICK.**
NIGHTS	NIGHTS	NIGHTS

WILLIE, BUDDY & PATRICK.
> WE BRAVED TOGETHER

WILLIE, BUDDY, PATRICK & WES.
> LIVE ON INSIDE OUR HEARTS.

WILLIE & INEZ.
> WE'VE GOT AN IRON BOND

WILLIE, INEZ, HENRI, PATRICK, FREDDY, WES, BUDDY & RICHARD.
> NO HATE COULD BREAK APART.

WILLIE, PATRICK, FREDDY, WES, BUDDY & RICHARD.
> NOW AND

WILLIE, INEZ, HENRI, PATRICK, FREDDY, WES, BUDDY & RICHARD.
> FOREVER,

WILLIE, PATRICK, FREDDY & WES.
> COME

WILLIE, INEZ, HENRI, PATRICK, FREDDY, WES, BUDDY & RICHARD.
> WHATEVER,

INEZ, HENRI, PATRICK, FREDDY, WES, BUDDY & RICHARD.
> YOU AND I.

WILLIE.
> THE NIGHTS WE BRAVED

	INEZ, HENRI &	
WILLIE.	**RICHARD.**	
TOGETHER	THE NIGHTS	**PATRICK & WES.**
	WE BRAVED	THE NIGHTS

WILLIE, INEZ, HENRI, PATRICK, WES & RICHARD.
LIVE ON INSIDE OUR HEARTS.

WILLIE.
WE'VE GOT AN IRON BOND NO HATE COULD BREAK
APART.
NOW AND

WILLIE, INEZ, HENRI, PATRICK, FREDDY, WES, BUDDY & RICHARD.
FOREVER,

WILLIE, PATRICK, FREDDY & WES.
COME

WILLIE, INEZ, HENRI, PATRICK, FREDDY, WES, BUDDY & RICHARD.
WHATEVER,

WILLIE.
YOU AND I.

INEZ, PATRICK & WES.
NOW AND FOREVER

WILLIE.
YOU AND I.

WILLIE, INEZ, HENRI, PATRICK, FREDDY, WES, BUDDY & RICHARD.
YOU AND I.

(The songs ends. Everyone in the bar applauds. **WILLIE** *embraces an audience member passionately.)*

WILLIE. Ohhhh! That was lovely. You know what this reminds me of?

RICHARD.	**BUDDY.**	**HENRI.**
Quick! Buddy, play another song!	Dear god.	NOOO!!

(The downstairs buzzer rings.)

FREDDY. Saved by the bell!

(The buzzer rings over and over again. **PATRICK**, *meanwhile, has started to notice the smell of gasoline from the stairwell.)*

HENRI. What the hell...?

BUDDY. Probably Dale again. Pay it no mind.

WILLIE. Come on. We were too hard on him.

INEZ. I don't think we did the right thing.

RICHARD. Let him back in. He belongs here.

BUDDY. Fine. If he wants to apologize, let him.

WILLIE. Well look at you!

PATRICK. Anybody smell gas?

BUDDY. Willie?

> (**WILLIE** *hisses at him in outrage.* **BUDDY** *motions to* **WES**.)

FREDDY. Come on Buddy! One more song!! Please please please.

BUDDY. I can't. My voice is shot, I've been singing since noon.

FREDDY. Don't worry. Wes will sing for you.

WES. What? I'm not a performer.

WILLIE. Everything about you is a performance!

> (*Door buzzes again.*)

[MUSIC NO. 14A "SOME KIND OF PARADISE (REPRISE)"]

WES. I'm not drunk enough for this!

BUDDY. Hey kid. Here. Put your your hand on top of mine.

> (*Everyone starts to gather around* **WES**, *cheering him on loudly.*)

WES.

I THINK I FOUND SOME KIND OF PARADISE
NO ANGEL WINGS –

FREDDY. Sing out Louise!

INEZ. *WEPA!*

> (*The buzzer rings over and over again, insistently.*)

WES.

OR FAIRY DUST. JUST THE RUSH OF LUST
BUT IT'S ALL RIGHT!

(The front door buzzes more, obnoxious and insistent.)

BUDDY. CAN SOMEONE OPEN THE GODDAMN DOOR?? HENRI!

HENRI. OKAY! JESUS CHRIST!

WES.

AND THOUGH THIS PLACE IS FAR FROM HEAVENLY
NO GOLDEN THRONE –
THE ECSTASY'S JUST TEMPORARY
BUT IT'S ALL RIGHT, BUT IT'S ALL –

*(**HENRI** heads downstairs, muttering to herself. While **WES** continues to sing, from offstage we hear the sounds of shattered glass. A fire breaks out in the staircase. We hear the wail of a fire alarm, piercing and loud. Even though **BUDDY** has stopped playing piano, the music continues to play against the alarm. **WES** immediately cups his hands over his ears in discomfort. The flames spread to the walls inside the bar. In contrast to the enveloping chaos, the **PATRONS** become expressionless and silent, as if frozen in time. **WES** panics, tries to shake them, but they don't respond.)*

What's happening??

*(As **PATRICK** delivers his monologue below, the **PATRONS** slowly exit down the stairs as their names are called. As he talks, the bar rapidly degenerates around them, until only a burned-out ruin is left. Present day.)*

PATRICK. The fire spread so quick. Henri opened the door. The oxygen fueled the gasoline and the staircase exploded. Suddenly the fire was everywhere. People started panicking and banging on the walls as if they'd break through somehow. Henri stumbled out into the street on fire, screaming and waving to try and get help. Inez was praying with Richard, right over there in the corner, while Freddy ran around trying to find another exit. But then there was too much smoke, so he grabbed his mom and they laid down underneath the piano and closed their eyes. Their bodies were found fused together.

WES. Stop... I don't want to hear any more. *Please.*

PATRICK. After the first five minutes, there wasn't much left of the staircase. Buddy helped Willie squeeze through the iron bars there on the window. He fell and died on impact, but Buddy only got halfway before getting stuck. He slowly burned to death as the people at the bar across the street watched. The police left his body in the window for a whole day before removing it, and when a reporter came to interview some of the people in the neighborhood later that night, a cab driver said, "At least it burned their dresses off."

WES. It's not true.

PATRICK. But it is.

WES. I don't understand...how could someone do that to you?

PATRICK. They never found out. No one cared. A year later, Dale shot himself.

WES. But you're still alive. I brought you back with me! Don't you see what this means?

PATRICK. They weren't able to identify my body. No one came forward and it was too badly burned. They buried me and two other unknown men in a potter's field.

> (**WES** *breaks down.* **PATRICK** *walks over and embraces him.*)
>
> (*There is a long silence.* **WES**' *grief turns to anger.*)

WES. This was all just some game to punish me. You want me to call it all off? Go bankrupt? Well you're too late. This place is being gutted next week, and no one will know what was here. That you were here. No one will remember.

PATRICK. *You* will remember. And one day you're gonna take everything you saw and twist it through your neurotic overly-complicated thought process and create something beautiful to put back into the world.

WES. I'll never find someone like you, any of you.

> (**PATRICK** *is heartsick but tries to smile through it.*)

PATRICK. You'll be okay. Look at how much you have to live for. This place is yours now! You have it so much better than –

WES. This shit isn't better! Nothing has changed. They're *killing* us. Orlando. Trans women. Ten-year-olds being bullied to death. And we just pretend it's not happening because every day there's a new shooting. Look at who's running this country! The people who spent their whole lives hating us and making us hate ourselves. Now they want us to all come together and hate – *anyone* who's different. We're putting kids in cages now. Our Vice President believes in conversion therapy. That's the world we live in! WE ARE NOT BETTER!

> (**PATRICK** *hugs* **WES.**)

PATRICK. You are. You will be.

WES. How do you know that?

PATRICK. Because I'm dead and fucking magical.

WES. I'm not ready for this to end.

PATRICK. Don't worry. We've always been here. We're not going anywhere.

> (*He disappears.*)

WES. PATRICK? ...PATRICK?

[MUSIC NO. 14B "PARADISE FRAGMENT"]

> (*Long beat as* **WES** *takes in the empty space. He goes to the piano and plunks out the notes of "Some Kind of Paradise" that Buddy taught him.*)

[MUSIC NO. 15 "THE VIEW UPSTAIRS"]

WES.

I TOLD YOU THE FUTURE WOULD BE GREAT
SO WON'T IT HURRY AND ARRIVE.
HOW LONG DO I HAVE TO WAIT?
HOW DO I GO BACK TO MY LIFE?
SMILE AND PRETEND I HAVE IT ALL:
A CLOSET OF CLOTHES I JUST LOOK AT
AND A PHONE FULL OF SUCH FABULOUS FRIENDS
WHO NEVER SEEM TO CALL.
TEN MILLION PEOPLE COULD FOLLOW ME
WOULD IT MAKE ME FEEL ANY LESS ALONE?
TO FILL THIS EMPTINESS, HOW MUCH MONEY DO I NEED?
AND IS IT WORTH, A LIFE SPENT ON MY OWN?

WITHOUT ANOTHER SOUL TO LEAN ON
A REASON TO CARE
AND ALL THOSE STUPID THINGS YOU DO IN LOVE.
I NEVER THOUGHT I HAD ENOUGH TO SHARE
BUT YOU SAW SOMETHING IN ME,
NOT BEYOND REPAIR AND I HOPE YOU WERE RIGHT;
THAT I WON'T LEAVE WITH ONLY TRAGEDY TONIGHT
'CAUSE THE ENDING'S STILL MINE,
THE ENDING'S STILL MINE TO WRITE.
STILL MINE TO WRITE.
IT'S NOT TOO LATE FOR ME TO CHANGE
IF I DON'T WASTE TIME ON BEING FAKE

I NEED SOMETHING THAT'S REAL.
I WANT TO FIND A FAM'LY.
NOT JUST THE ONE I GREW UP WITH,
BUT THE ONE I'LL CHOOSE TO MAKE.

AND IN A WORLD FULL OF DARKNESS
WE CREATE OUR OWN PARADISE.
'CAUSE I'VE GAINED A SECOND-SIGHT
FOUND LOVE AND HAD IT STOLEN THE SAME NIGHT
BUT THE ENDING'S STILL MINE
THE ENDING'S STILL MINE TO WRITE.
STILL MINE TO WRITE.

WES.	OTHERS.
IT'S STILL MINE TO WRITE.	OOH
IT'S STILL MINE TO WRITE.	OOH

(The spirits of the UpStairs Lounge come back once more to join **WES**, *now dressed in seventies-inspired couture from his debut fashion collection: brilliant, breathtaking, and alive. They walk the runway of his fashion show, each striking a different pose like a spread in* Vanity Fair. *When* **WES** *finally sees* **PATRICK**, *there is some special acknowledgement – perhaps* **WES** *adjusts his jacket, pins a brooch to his lapel, or maybe it's just a look of gratitude.)*

WES.

WES.	INEZ, HENRI, FREDDY, PATRICK & WILLIE.	BUDDY, RICHARD & DALE.
AND THE NIGHTS WE BRAVED TOGETHER LIVE ON		
INSIDE OUR HEARTS	I THINK I FOUND SOME KIND OF	I THINK I FOUND SOME KIND OF
WE'VE GOT AN IRON BOND NO HATE COULD	PARADISE	PARADISE
BREAK APART NOW AND	I THINK I FOUND SOME KIND OF	I THINK I FOUND SOME KIND OF
FOREVER, COME	I THINK I FOUND SOME KIND	PARADISE
WHATEVER	OF	OF
NOW AND	I THINK I FOUND SOME KIND OF	I THINK I FOUND SOME KIND OF
FOREVER, COME WHATEVER	PARADISE	PARADISE

WES.	INEZ, HENRI, FREDDY, PATRICK & WILLIE.	BUDDY, RICHARD & DALE.

NOW AND
  FOREVER
	I THINK I FOUND
	  SOME KIND
	  OF
		I THINK I FOUND
		  SOME KIND
		  OF

	I THINK I FOUND
	  SOME KIND
	  OF
		PARADISE

COME WHATEVER

INEZ, HENRI, BUDDY, RICHARD & DALE.
PARADISE

FREDDY, PATRICK & WILLIE.
PARADISE

WES.	FREDDY, PATRICK & WILLIE.	INEZ, HENRI, BUDDY, RICHARD & DALE.

NOW AND
  FOREVER
	FOREVER	NOW AND
		  FOREVER

COME		
WHATEVER	WHATEVER	WHATEVER
YOU AND I	YOU AND I	YOU AND I

(The bar lights of the UpStairs Lounge swell and the destroyed space for one moment becomes beautiful again.)

(Blackout.)

The End